KIDS EXPLORE AMERICA'S HISPANIC HERITAGE

Westridge Young Writers Workshop

John Muir Publications
Santa Fe, New Mexico

Read this book and you will learn.
We, as all people, make the world turn.
Each person is different in his own special way.
We want you to know that that's okay.
You can learn from these people as you will see.
This book is for you—given from me!

This book is dedicated to people of different cultures, with the hope
that they are proud of who they are.

John Muir Publications, P.O. Box 613, Santa Fe, NM 87504

© 1992 by Jefferson County School District No. R-1
Cover © 1992 by John Muir Publications
All rights reserved. Published 1992
Printed in the United States of America

First edition. Third printing January 1993

Library of Congress Cataloging-in-Publication Data
Kids explore America's Hispanic heritage / Westridge Young Writers
Workshop. — 1st ed.
     p.   cm.
     Includes index.
     Summary: Presents writings by students in grades three to seven on
topics of Hispanic culture, including dance, cooking, games,
history, art, songs, and role models.
     ISBN 1-56261-034-1
     1. Hispanic Americans—Juvenile literature.   2. Children's
writings, American.   [1. Hispanic Americans.   2. Children's
writings.] I. Westridge Young Writers Workshop.
     E184.S75K53   1992
     973'.0468—dc20
                                                               91-42232
                                                               CIP
                                                               AC

Design   Susan Surprise
Typefaces   Garamond and Triumvirate
Typesetter   Copygraphics, Inc.
Printer   Banta Company

Distributed to the book trade by
W.W. Norton & Co., Inc.
New York, New York

Distributed to the education market by
The Wright Group
19201 120th Avenue N.E.
Bothell, Washington 98011-9512

Photo Credits   Photos on pages 13, 14, 15, 18, 19, 24, and 38 courtesy of
Denver Public Library Western History Department.
Photo on page 11 courtesy of Colorado Historical Society.

CONTENTS

ACKNOWLEDGMENTS

We, the eighty-two student authors, are especially thankful to the people of Hispanic background who shared their time, talents, history, and knowledge with us while we were writing this book. We would also like to thank the Westridge Elementary School staff, the Westridge PTA, Ron Horn, Rose Roy, Josh Herald, Ruth Maria Acevedo, and all of our teachers for their confidence in us young writers.

Special thanks go to several businesses and organizations for their financial support. Student scholarships were donated by King Soopers, Denver, Colorado, and Lakewood Civitan Club, Lakewood, Colorado. Teacher scholarships were donated by Adolph Coor's Company, Golden, Colorado. We want to thank Pam Faro, Storyteller, Lafayette, Colorado; Our Lady of Guadalupe Dancers, Our Lady of Guadalupe Catholic Church, Denver, Colorado; Ron Rich, Publisher of Booktalk, Lakewood, Colorado; and Candy's Tortilla, Denver, Colorado, for their donations of services and supplies. Thanks also to the IBM Corporation for donating computers on which we did word processing.

STUDENTS' PREFACE

I'm proud to be me.
'Cause that's who I am.
Be proud to be you,
'Cause that's who you are.
The differences 'tween us,
Help us all to grow.
They strengthen our hearts,
So our pride we can show.
Respect all others and they'll respect you.
Be kind to everyone in all that you do.
What's in this book you will need to know,
If you want to learn, if you want to grow.
Explore different cultures or maybe your own,
As we teach you of customs and stories well known.
Through the eyes of a child you're about to be taught,
And to your surprise you may learn quite a lot.

This book is fun, interesting, and cool, and it's from a kid's point of view! We, the eighty-two authors, are students in grades three through seven. We feel it was worth using part of our summer to write *Kids Explore America's Hispanic Heritage* instead of just watching T.V. or riding bikes. We are excited because this book will be available all over the United States, and it will help Americans enjoy a unique part of their heritage.

This book is not just for kids. *Kids Explore America's Hispanic Heritage* is a great opportunity for everyone to learn. We've opened the door and given you just a peek into one culture.

TEACHERS' PREFACE

A dream is only a dream,
Until you take action
And make it reality.
This dream was the hard work of many.

Many people may wonder how this book came about. It was conceived at Westridge Elementary School, located in Jefferson County, a western suburb of Denver, Colorado. Book publishing is a well-established part of the school curriculum. John Muir Publications of Santa Fe, New Mexico, was enthusiastic about our idea for a series of books, all written by children, on different cultures within the United States. These books, part of a projected PROUD TO BE series, are meant to be informative as well as to instill a sense of pride in our diverse heritage.

We developed the plans for this volume in a summer enrichment class. During that class, students were exposed to the various aspects of Hispanic heritage about which they later wrote. They learned about dances, cooking, games, history, art, songs, and real people. They researched, worked on word processing, illustrated, organized, wrote, and proofread. Soon, students will move into publicity and marketing and will present programs to other schools.

While students enhanced their writing skills and acquired firsthand knowledge of Hispanic culture, we earned college credits through a course entitled "Integrating Hispanic Studies into the School Curriculum." Most of us are Hispanic, and our interest in learning more about our own culture fueled enthusiasm within the whole group. We all explored ways to integrate Hispanic culture into the curriculum and improved our knowledge of publishing procedures and the process of writing. It was our goal to produce a book that would be a valuable addition to school libraries and programs.

The students, a majority of whom are Hispanic, are from the Jefferson County Schools. They represent diverse economic and cultural backgrounds. Scholarship funds were available from the business community for those students who needed them.

Four book-length publications have already emerged from our writing labs and are being sold commercially. They are available in Colorado bookstores under the following titles: *As Kids See Denver*, *Just My Luck*, *Colorado Kids Dig Up the Past*, and *Explore Colorado—Kid Style*. *Just My Luck* is being distributed internationally. Our students love being full-fledged authors and basking in the limelight that publication generates. They are proud to be a part of this book!

HISTORY OF HISPANICS IN AMERICA

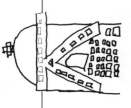

Important people sculpting our land.
Fighting, exploring, lending a band.
Help us hold on to our past
While we reach into the future
And build it to last.

Welcome to Hispanic history. We will look into some of the events and people of Hispanic culture from the 1400s to the present. Starting in the 1400s, the century when the Spanish explorers came to the New World, can give us a clearer picture of how the Hispanic traditions found their way to our country. History can be fun, especially when we realize how history, like America's Hispanic heritage, matters to each of us in America today.

When real historians, people who study the past, write history books, they use many sources of information and sometimes spend years doing research. They use old diaries written by people long ago. They look through other books that describe the past. They go through old pictures and photographs. They talk to old people who made history. Through these many ways, they try to piece together what life was like in the past. We have tried to be good historians. Our book covers many important people and events. If you are interested by one or more of these, the library is a terrific place to find out more information. If this part of our book gets you more interested in the history that shaped America's Hispanic heritage, we are excited!

In this brief history, we hope you will see how these events and people have brought together the Spanish and native groups and blended them into the Hispanic heritage of our country. We will use

Mesa Verde in Colorado, a site of ancient Anasazi civilization

the Aztecs to show an example of one native civilization. We will share how the Taínos of Cuba interacted with Columbus so you can understand how complicated the Spanish takeover of land in the New World really was. Then we will look at other explorers from Spain and how the very different cultures related to each other. We will talk about the missionaries and how they treated the Indians. Next we will get into the period when the United States became a country and needed more land. We will see how this changed the lives of the Mexican people who lived in the United States and made Mexico look at the United States a little more carefully.

We will look at people who fought for Hispanic rights. Cuba and Puerto Rico, both important to the Hispanics in America, will be reviewed as important parts of American history, too. Last, we will see a lot of Hispanic people who are making names for themselves in the United States today.

THE MEETING OF DIFFERENT CULTURES

The ancestors of Hispanic people came from many different cultures. These very different cultures, which had been devel-

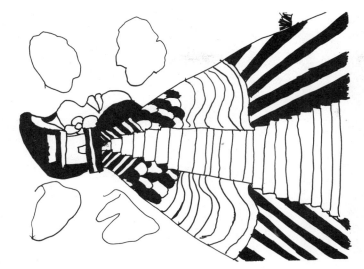

oping for many hundreds of years, lived in different parts of the world thousands of miles from each other.

One of the original cultures of today's Hispanic people is the native people of the Americas. You may know these native people as Indians. Some of the natives that influenced Hispanic culture lived in what is now Mexico, Cuba, Central America, the West Indies, and the United States. For thousands of years, these people lived in groups with their own traditions, values, and religious beliefs. In fact, many Indian cultures began in prehistoric time. Later on, other Indian cultures, like the Aztecs of Mexico, the Incas of South America, the Maya of Central America, the Arawaks of Puerto Rico, and the Tainos of Cuba, developed in this area. History shows that these Indians were very smart in agriculture and hunting, but they also did great things in astronomy, mathematics, architecture, and many other difficult subjects.

The Aztecs were a very advanced culture for their time, which was from around A.D. 1100 to the 1520s. (A.D. means after Christ died. The year Christ died was the year 0.) The Aztecs built tall buildings, like pyramids. They mined gold, silver, jade, and turquoise. Their capital city was Tenochtitlán (ten-och-teat-LON). It was built on land that was once a lake. The Aztecs drained the lake and filled it back up with dirt. Ever since this time this area has had a great number of earthquakes because the ground is still unstable. Today, Mexico City is built right on top of the old city of Tenochtitlán.

Warning: FOR STRONG STOMACHS ONLY! The Aztecs believed that to keep the sun moving across the sky, they needed to offer up to it something from a human body that moved all the time. So, the Aztecs offered the beating heart that was taken quickly from sacrificial victims during a complicated religious ceremony.

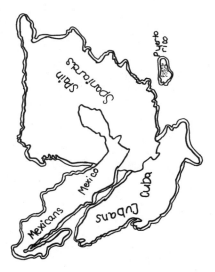

east on a ship. (Guess where the Spanish come in.)

There have been many different explorers in this region. Explorers are people who have taken risks and have gone somewhere they didn't know much about. Can you imagine talking the president of the United States into letting you take a space ship for days and days to travel to another planet? This is what it may have been like for early explorers.

Some people don't like to call the Spanish "explorers" because the Indians were already living here. The Indians may have thought of the Spanish as invaders, and we can see their point. We will refer to the Spanish as explorers, but we will try to share the truth about their travels as they really did act more like invaders. Because the explorers were from Spain, many areas in the Western Hemisphere speak Spanish today.

The Aztecs felt they could use human sacrifices to take away the sins of the people.

The Aztecs also had some really cool sounding names for their gods. Did you know that Quetzalcoat (ket-sul-KO-ah-tul) created mankind? That's what the Aztecs thought. They built temples in his honor. Quetzalcoatl was shown in drawings with a serpent head and a bird body. The word "Quetzalcoatl" means plumed serpent. The Aztecs also knew him as the god of wisdom. He told the ancestors of the Aztec people to stop sacrificing humans and start sacrificing animals. The people didn't like that and told him to leave. He said he would return from the

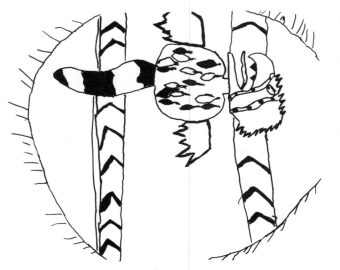

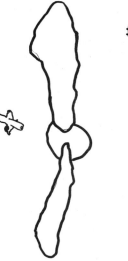

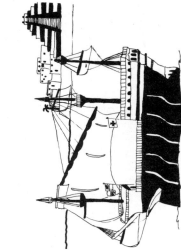

In the 1400s, explorers from Spain started to cross the ocean and discover that there were civilizations of people living in the part of the world that we call Mexico, Central America, and the West Indies. Christopher Columbus, whose Spanish name was Cristóbal Colon, was one of these explorers, and he wanted to go across the Atlantic Ocean to find an easier way to get to the Indies. This is what we call India and Southeast Asia today. If the Spanish wanted to trade with India by traveling west, they had to pay every country on the way there a fee to pass through their lands. This could get very expensive! Instead, Columbus wished to find an easier way to travel around the world on the ocean. Some people thought he was crazy because they thought the world was flat and when he got to the end he would fall off. This must not have bothered him much, because he was excited to make the voyage no matter what.

Columbus had been a map maker for the country of Portugal. History books tell us that he may have known about the Portuguese voyages to the New World earlier in the 1400s, even though they had tried to keep it a secret so they could have their own trade routes. Because of this, he was probably real confident about his plan to sail to the Indies.

Columbus got his supplies for sailing from King Ferdinand and Queen Isabella of Spain. When Columbus set off on his voyage, others didn't know if he would make it. This is where the rhyme comes in: "In fourteen hundred and ninety-two, Columbus sailed the ocean blue." Instead of reaching his destination, Columbus found a new world.

Christopher Columbus never realized that North and South America would be in his way to get to India, which is where he really wanted to go. Instead, his first journey ended up in what is now known as the West Indies. Some historians say Columbus thought he was in India, so he called the people he met "Indians."

The king and queen of Spain were surprised and excited about Columbus's claims. They hoped Columbus would find gold or goods that they could make money from and ship back to Spain, so they sent him again.

THE WORLD

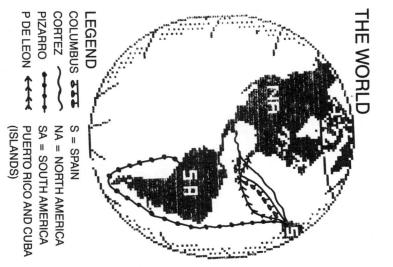

LEGEND

COLUMBUS ᔓᔓᔓ
CORTEZ ●●●
PIZARRO ●●●
P DE LEON ➤➤➤

S = SPAIN
NA = NORTH AMERICA
SA = SOUTH AMERICA
PUERTO RICO AND CUBA (ISLANDS)

Juan Ponce de Leon went on Columbus's second trip to the New World in 1493. They landed on the shores of an island, and because of the riches they hoped to find there, they called it Puerto Rico. This means "rich port" in Spanish. Here the Spanish met the Taino Indians who lived in parts of Puerto Rico and Cuba with their relatives, the Arawaks.

There were many differences between the Spanish and the natives. First of all, the Spanish felt that they had to own things. That's why they made claim to territory. The native groups believed the land couldn't belong to anyone, that it was just part of nature. This is why the Indians didn't understand why the Spaniards wanted to claim the land.

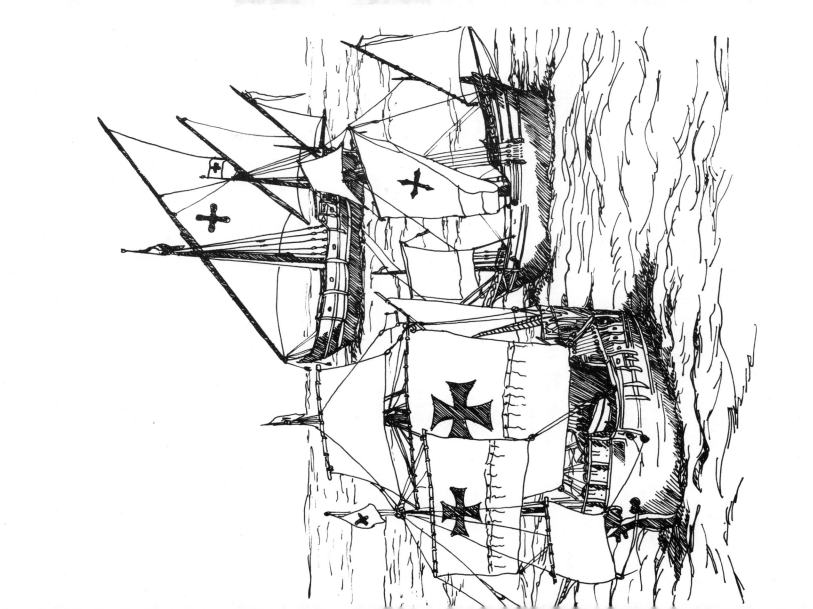

Another difference was how they felt about gold. For example, the Tainos told Ponce de Leon about the rivers of gold because whenever he heard the word "gold" he would get excited. They told him there was lots of gold all over the place, even though it wasn't true. The Tainos didn't understand how important gold was to Ponce de Leon. It was not very special to the Tainos, so they didn't understand why he became so mean when he couldn't find it. Ponce de Leon had the natives mine for the gold.

Problems came up between the Spanish and the natives. Taino weapons were useless against the Spaniards. Just as in Cuba, many Tainos were killed in battle, and a lot also died from the diseases the Spanish brought with them. Measles,

tuberculosis, and smallpox did not exist in the New World until the people from Europe brought them. If the natives didn't die from the diseases or in battles, they died from working in the mines all day and all night. In fact, in Cuba and Puerto Rico together, more than eight million Taino Indians died. So many died that the Spanish found there weren't enough workers. Soon the Spanish brought in slaves from Africa to work.

The diaries and writings of others such as Father Bartolome de las Casas show that many cruel things happened to the native groups of people Columbus and his men met. The last six years of the 1400s are known as the Black Legend in Spanish history. Columbus and his brothers were governors in Cuba. They ruled and were mean to the Tainos. Some were tortured for not following the Spanish laws, which they didn't understand. They might have had a hand cut off as a penalty.

Many things like this also happened when other Spanish and European explorers settled the New World. More details about Columbus can be found in his ship's log, which is translated into English, and the diaries and reports of other explorers and missionaries.

In 1509, Ponce de Leon became governor of Puerto Rico, making it a Spanish colony. From Puerto Rico, Ponce de Leon sailed to some other islands to make his claim of Hispaniola, now known as Haiti and the Dominican Republic. Ponce de Leon did leave his mark on Puerto Rico, because today one of the largest cities in Puerto Rico is named Ponce.

In 1519, another Spanish explorer called Hernan Cortés came looking for gold. When he arrived in Mexico, the Aztecs remembered the legend of Quetzalcoatl, the man who had the serpent's head and a bird's body. Quetzalcoatl left the Aztecs and said he would return on a ship but that when he came back he would have light skin and a beard. So when Cortés arrived, the Aztecs thought he and his men were gods. They gave him gold and jewels and lots of respect. When one of Cortés's men was hurt and blood came out of his injury, the Aztecs began to wonder if Cortés was really a god. Cortés soon wore out his welcome. He was cruel to the Aztecs. He took advantage of the Aztecs' kindness and started to demand gold and treasure—even more gold than a god would need. He would punish the Aztecs if they didn't move or work to dig for gold as fast as he told them. Sometimes he would snip off the tips of their noses or tips of their ears if they disobeyed him. The Aztec leader sent a message for Cortés to leave, but Cortés didn't want to.

Many groups who were enemies of the Aztecs joined Cortés in a great battle against them. The Aztecs had clubs, spears, and axes. The Spanish had weapons that were high-tech for their time, so Cortés and the Spanish beat the Aztecs and captured the city of Tenochtitlán in 1521.

Alvarar Nuñez Cabeza de Vaca was another Spanish conqueror who was on an expedition to capture Indians to make them slaves for the Spanish. He was shipwrecked in the Gulf of Mexico in 1528 and accidentally became an explorer when

Americans remember Ponce de Leon because he explored and named Florida (Place of Flowers). He was looking for a really neat fountain. The legend said if you drank or bathed from this special fountain, you would stay young forever and ever. This fountain was called the Fountain of Youth. Did Ponce de Leon find this fountain in 1513 when he disappeared, or did he bite the dust?

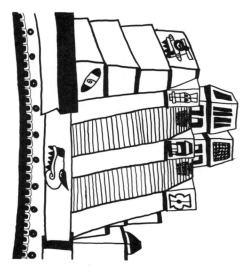

he was just trying to save his life. He walked from Indian group to Indian group trying to get home. Cabeza de Vaca would have died if the Indians hadn't helped him. He heard over and over from the Indians their stories about the golden riches north of Mexico. (Remember that the Indians didn't think about gold the same way the Spaniards did.) Cabeza de Vaca was very sick, so he did not go after the gold. When he got better, he went back to Mexico and told the Spanish leaders the stories of gold. Cabeza de Vaca knew that the Spaniards would always look for the gold he had told them about. He also knew that the people who had helped him would be made into slaves to find the gold. He ended up hurting the people who had been kind to him and had helped him stay alive. He was very sad for a long time because of what had happened to the Indians who had helped him.

"Gold! Gold! Gold! I want to find the Seven Cities of Gold!" cried Francisco de Coro-

nado, another Spanish explorer. Coronado was the first white man to travel around what we now call the southwestern United States. He brought horses to the natives so that the slaves could do more work in the fields and also brought smallpox, which wiped out many of the Indians. He had heard of the seven cities in the northern part of Mexico, now America, that were made out of gold. He was disappointed when he found the small Indian villages in the areas now known as Arizona, New Mexico, Colorado, and Kansas. He never found the cities made of gold. When he came back to Mexico, nobody thought he was a real explorer because he never found what he had gone looking for.

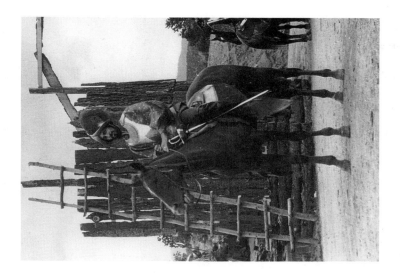

The Spanish had to do something for a money system. Some of the first mints, places where coins are made by the government, were built by the Spanish. With all the silver and gold the native people were mining, the time was right to make coins. At first, in the 1500s and 1600s, the coins were made very roughly by beating out a thin stamp of silver or gold into a shape that had the Spanish royal coat of arms. These rough coins are known as Cobbs and can still be found on the ocean floor from many sunken ships off the coast of Florida, the Caribbean, and all over the Gulf of Mexico. Many of the ships were often loaded very heavily trying to take as much treasure as possible back to Spain. There are even treasure hunter museums today where many of these old treasures can be seen.

The coin presses grew, and Spain minted its famous eight reales (ray-ALL-ace) starting in the early 1700s. Spain had mints in its homeland, in Mexico, and all over South America and put different marks on the coins telling where they were made. When people just couldn't get the right change to buy or sell something, they just chopped these coins up like a pizza into smaller pieces. This is where the words two bits, four bits, and pieces of eight come from.

Many of these eight reales, also called pillar dollars, made their way all over the United States and were used as money because early American currency was often hard to get. Early colonists in the northern United States used this currency.

THE MOVE NORTH

For many reasons, the people of the Middle Americas were urged to move to the north. The Spanish claimed the territory that included the present states of California, Nevada, Utah, Colorado, New Mexico, Arizona, and Texas. In 1821, Mexico declared its freedom from Spain, so the Mexican flag flew over this area. However, the Mexicans began to lose their land in the 1840s. In less than fifty years, the land that is now the southwestern part of the United States had changed hands three times. This all began when the Spanish moved north.

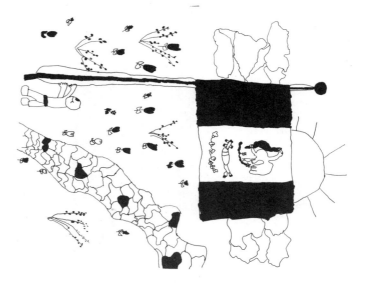

Some Spaniards wanted more land, some wanted gold, and some wanted to spread Christianity. The Spanish also moved north because there was not much food in the south. There were people already living in the area to the north of present-day Mexico.

The people moving to the north had to develop a plan. They decided to build villages. They used adobe bricks to make houses called haciendas (ah-see-EN-dahs). A presidio was built in each village as a fort where soldiers could stay to watch over the church and the Spaniards. The Spanish forced the natives to build missions so that they could bring their own people to live there. In return, the Spanish promised to use the mission to protect the Indians from other native groups that weren't

friendly with them. One of the problems was that there weren't many unfriendly natives around for the Indians in the missions to be afraid of. Some of the native groups in the Americas, now the United States, didn't fight with each other. They had nothing to fight about. They lived just fine together. That's why the Spaniards had to force the native groups to build the missions. Most Indians did not own land or territory or have any interest in gold until the Europeans made it important. A few warlike tribes fought over natural resources, but they were the exception.

One of the goals of missions was to convert the native people to Christianity. The missionaries did this in many ways.

To be a mission Indian was awful. The Spaniards brought the Indians to the mission, usually by force. Once the Indians were in the missions, they were not allowed to leave. The Indians were baptized and converted to the Catholic religion. In the missions, the Indians had to do the farming, building, weaving, and

The missions were very important in settling the land that the explorers claimed. Some people aren't sure if the missionaries really did help the people who had lived there before the missionaries came.

The first colony in what is now the southwestern United States was built by Juan de Oñate. The king of Spain gave Oñate permission to take some people from Mexico with him to the land that is now known as New Mexico. The people he took included Spanish soldiers, natives, missionaries, and mestizos. (Mestizos are people who have one parent who is Spanish and one parent who is Indian.) By 1630, there were twenty-five missions around New Mexico. Oñate became the governor of Sante Fe. He called his place

blacksmithing. If they tried to escape, the Spanish treated them cruelly. The Spanish might even cut off a foot or a hand or smash an ankle to keep them from running away.

The way the Indians had lived before the Spanish came was very different from the way they lived in the missions. Their food was really different from what they were used to. There was less space, and there were more people. Their rooms were tiny and not very clean. It was a real bad situation. The new diseases brought to them made the Indians weak, and they got sick a lot. Over half of the native people in the missions died from smallpox or bubonic plague. Look at it this way. If you had four people in your family, two or three might die.

Depiction of the Spanish discovery of the Mississippi River in May 1541

of government El Palacio de los Goberna-dores, or Palace of the Governors.

Father Junipero Serra was a mission-ary in California. In the 1700s, he helped the people build missions to live in. San Francisco, Los Angeles, and San Diego were a few of the twenty-one missions established along a route called El Camino Real, the Royal Road, a path connecting all of the missions. Later, this path was named U.S. 101, a major highway along the California coast.

Aianasio Dominguez and Silvestre Velez de Escalante were two missionaries who traveled together in 1776. They left what we now call Santa Fe, New Mexico, to travel through Colorado, Utah, Arizona,

and New Mexico to find new paths to Cali-fornia. They never made it to California. They thought teaching Christianity to the Indians they met along the way was more important. They also kept a diary of what they saw each day. From reading their diary, their trip sounded very challenging.

Dominguez and Escalante's expedi-tion ran into many problems. Sometimes the weather wasn't good. Sometimes the trails were very rough. One time they shared some food with the Sabuagana Yutas Indians. One Indian ate so much that he got sick. He started to blame Domin-guez and Escalante and their men, who were afraid that they would be in danger if the Indians found out about the stomple who are not Hispanic) came into the Mexican territories, they did all right. Many of them learned the language, converted to the Catholic religion, and got along with the people who lived there. When more Anglos came, Mexico started to lose control in the present U.S. Southwest. The ways of the American merchants and trappers didn't mix with the ways of the Mexicans. The customs and traditions of the different people in this area were very confusing to everyone. The native Mexicans were concerned with the useless killing and hunting that the American merchants and trappers did. Americans who came into the area were often aggressive. The Mexicans were humble and more formal. Most Mexicans were very careful with nature and respected it more than some Americans.

Because of these differences, fighting began in 1835. The Anglos believed the land we call Texas should be theirs. The Anglos started taking over small military

Spanish discovery of the Colorado River in 1540

ach problem. But the Indian who had eaten too much finally threw up. Then he felt better and everything was fine again.

One special priest named Miguel Hidalgo lived in the 1800s. He wanted to help the Indians in Mexico, so he taught them to grow their own crops and to do things for themselves. He and the Indians went to Mexico City to get away from the Spanish soldiers. Father Hidalgo got captured and was killed. Now the Mexicans believe he was very important, so he is called the Father of Mexico.

After a lot of conflict between Mexico and Spain, Mexico declared its freedom and independence. So in 1821, the Mexican flag flew over this area.

At first, when the Anglos (white peo-

The Alamo was built in 1836. This is how it looks today in San Antonio, Texas.

places from the Mexicans. Then in December of 1835, the Anglos took the Alamo, a military building in San Antonio. The president of Mexico said this action was unfair. He sent troops across the Rio Grande to get the land back for Mexico because he felt the Anglos had no business being there. The Mexicans attacked the Alamo and took control. While they were resting after the battle, another Texan army surprised them. More than 600 Mexican soldiers were killed in the Battle of San Jacinto on April 21, 1836. After this, Texas became an independent republic. This was

the beginning of Mexico losing its valued lands to the north.

MODERN PROBLEMS AND RESPONSES

Problems about land had been building up for years because the United States wanted to move its boundaries all the way to the Pacific Ocean. The United States had tried to make a deal to buy part of northern Mexico, but Mexico did not want to sell it. This started the Mexican-American War.

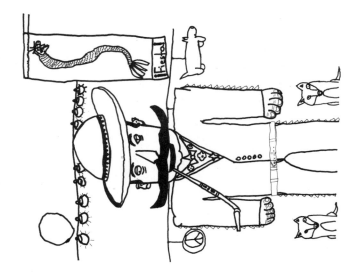

There was no way the president of Mexico and his people could protect the Mexican territory that they had lived in all their lives. In a year, Mexico had lost the lands that are now the states of California, Nevada, Utah, New Mexico, Colorado, Wyoming, and parts of Arizona. The United States was larger than Mexico after gaining this land. The Treaty of Guadalupe Hidalgo in 1848 ended the Mexican-American War. By the terms of the treaty, the United States gained one-third of Mexico. The Hispanics who lived in the area that used to be Mexico were suddenly living in the United States. Many of the Anglo-Americans did not respect these new Mexican residents. The Americans disobeyed the promises of the treaty. They did not give the Hispanics full citizenship and property rights, and they would not let them speak their own language, Spanish. The Anglo-Americans discouraged the Hispanics from having their own religion, culture, and customs.

Many of the American laws did not seem fair to the Hispanics and other non-Anglos. Anglo-Americans treated the new residents unfairly by telling the Hispanics the American laws in English. The Hispanics did not understand this language, so lots of times they were cheated out of their land. The Hispanic people were often so confused about what was going on that the Anglos took advantage of them.

One of the laws that was unfair to Hispanics and to black Americans did not allow them to be on a jury. This law lasted until 1954. Some states made it illegal to speak Spanish in schools. Before the Bilingual Education Act in 1968, children couldn't be taught in any language but English. So if they only spoke Spanish, it was too bad! Until 1970, a law in California said that you had to be able to read the Constitution in English before you could vote. People had to take a test in English before they could vote. That wasn't fair!

Another example of prejudice occurred in 1946. Zoot suits were then popular among young Mexican-American men. Zoot suit pants had a high waistline and were tapered at the ankles. The long suit jackets came down to the knees. Zoot suits were very popular in California as well as other parts of the United States. But being part of a group was not always good for Mexican-American men. Once, sailors on leave in California attacked Mexican-Americans in zoot suits. Police did nothing to stop the sailors from beating up the young zoot suiters. The newspapers reported that the zoot suiters had started violent riots and the zoot suiters were arrested. Again, unfair! The government wouldn't listen to the growing Hispanic problems. This made the Hispanics feel helpless and angry.

Hispanic workers had generally not been treated well on the job. One of the most difficult jobs was to work as a migrant worker. Migrant workers are people who move from area to area, crop to crop, picking fruit and vegetables for small wages. The Spanish word for them is *brazeros* (brah-SAY-ros), which means people who work with their arms. These migrant workers often have to travel because the growing season changes and

Migrant farm worker

they need to search for a new job when they finish harvesting the fruit, vegetables, or crops in one area. Not only is the work hard but the houses are overcrowded and not good. There are no doctors for them if they get sick. Migrants tried to organize as early as 1883. Vaqueros (vah-KEHR-rohs), Mexican-American cowboys, organized a strike for better pay in Texas that same year. Between 1900 and 1930, Mexican-Americans led or took part in miners' strikes.

Cesar Chavez and his family were migrant workers. He knew Hispanics needed to get organized. They needed leadership. For example, when the Mexican-American migrant workers tried to earn money and get a better life in the

United States, business owners were often unfair to them. They had the migrant workers do the work but then paid them very little money. Sometimes they didn't pay them at all. Hispanics knew something had to be done to help improve the living conditions of their people. They needed to get together and decide what to do about their problems in the United States.

Cesar Chavez

Cesar Chavez didn't like the way migrant workers were treated. He started the National Farm Workers Association in 1962. This was a union to get better pay. Did you know that Cesar Chavez once didn't eat for 36 days? He didn't eat be-

cause he was protesting the poor living conditions the braceros lived in. He wanted to show people that he was serious, so he went on a hunger strike. The other important thing he did was to turn around the meaning of the word "Chicano" so people would understand it better. Chicano used to be one of the worst words a person could use to refer to a Mexican person.

Protest in Denver

As the parents of Hispanic children wanted to fit into Anglo-American society and even forget their past heritage, their children joined together by calling themselves "Chicanos." Instead of trying to mix into the Anglo way of life, these children adopted an identity they felt proud of.

Other Hispanic workers tried to join unions for better treatment and better pay, but some unions did not accept them. So, the Hispanics formed their own union called the Confederación de Uniones Obreras Mexicanos (Confederation of Unions of Mexican Workers, CUOM). By doing this, they were making themselves stronger and protesting against the people who were unfair to them. In 1929, a group of Hispanics formed a group called the League of United Latin American Citizens (LULAC). They wanted to help Hispanic people be good, patriotic citizens, learn English, get more education, and be treated equally. LULAC still exists today.

OTHER ORIGINS OF HISPANIC CULTURE

Do you know all the places where you will find the Hispanic culture? Well, read on. Cuba is a big island that is 746 miles long. That's almost the same as the distance from New York to Chicago. Cuba was a Spanish colony for a long time because of the Spanish explorers who landed there. That's why a lot of their culture and customs are Hispanic.

In the early 1960s, many Cubans came to the United States because their country's government was changing and they didn't agree with the changes they were going to have to live with if they stayed. Many came to Miami, Florida, just 90 miles away. Imagine having to choose between staying with your family and friends or leaving your country for a new one. One person who did this is Tino Mendez, who was seventeen years old when he left Cuba for freedom in the United States. Look for his story in the Real People section of this book.

Puerto Rico is a small island off the coast of Florida. The island itself is only 100 miles by 35 miles and about the size of Connecticut. Puerto Ricans have been citizens of the United States since 1917. Puerto Rico is a commonwealth of the United States. That means it's almost like a state. Puerto Rico never did live up to its name of being a "rich port." Many people had to move to the mainland in the 1960s because of problems with hunger and finding jobs. The first to come to the mainland of the United States were garment workers, people who make clothes for a living. They mostly went to New York because they got the best jobs there. Over two million Puerto Ricans live in this country, and half of them live in New York. New York's Puerto Rican population is second only to Puerto Rico's capital, San Juan. Read about Bishop Roberto Gonzales and Doctor Carlos Flores, two Puerto Rican-Americans, in the Real People section of our book.

HISPANIC LEADERS

Hispanics have always been eager to serve America in the military. They have received many honors for their military service. They have won more medals than any other minority group in World War II. This is really something to be proud of!

Private José P. Martinez was part of the Seventh Army Division that fought World War II. He won the Congressional Medal of Honor for saving the lives of the men in his unit in a battle in Japan. We visited his statue while writing this book. He was a true war hero.

Many Hispanics served in World War II and earned the special benefits offered to all those who served in the war. These special benefits were part of the G.I. Bill, which gives veterans (people who had

Statue honoring Pvt. José P. Martinez, Denver, Colorado

been soldiers) the chance to go to college, buy homes, and start businesses. After using their benefits from the G.I. Bill, Hispanics organized themselves to use their skills to help their communities. This group is called the American G.I. Forum.

There are other Hispanic people who are trying to make change happen for their fellow Hispanics in American. They have worked to elect Hispanics to all levels of politics, such as the office of mayor, governor, and Congress. Some people do not know that there are Hispanics in government positions or other high places.

Hispanics have earned many "firsts" for their people. Lauro Cavazos became the first Hispanic Secretary of Education. Manuel Lujan became the first Hispanic Secretary of the Interior. Katherine Davalos Ortega was the first Hispanic Treasurer of the United States.

A few examples of successful Hispanic politicians are Ilena Ros-Lehtinen, a U.S. Representative from Florida; Rebecca Vigil-Giron, New Mexico's Secretary of State; and Jose Serrano, a New York State Representative. Other Hispanic politicians include former Denver Mayor Federico Pena; Dan Morales, a Texas State Representative; Jerry Apodaca, a former governor of New Mexico; and Raul Castro, a former governor of Arizona.

Of course, there are many Hispanics who have made a difference outside of government, including Cesar Chavez, who is mentioned earlier.

Would you like to be an awesome, trained astronaut? Franklin Chang-Diaz and Sidney Gutierrez said yes. They entered the astronaut training program in the 1980s and became astronauts working with NASA space projects.

Here, for all you sports fans, are some more popular Hispanics that you might recognize. Tom Flores was a head coach for the Los Angeles Raiders and became the general manager of the Seattle Seahawks. Lou Piniella became the manager of the Cincinnati Reds. Jose Torres, a former world champion, became the New York Commissioner of Boxing. Jim Plunkett won the Heisman Trophy in college football and was the quarterback for the world champion Raiders. He was Ron Rivera's hero, and Ron himself became a professional football player for the Chicago Bears.

Max Montoya and Anthony Muñoz became great National Football League stars. The three Zendejas brothers (Luis, Max, and Tony) all kicked for NFL teams. Luis played for the Philadelphia Eagles, Max played for the Houston Oilers, and Tony played for the Green Bay Packers.

Fernando Valenzuela earned millions of dollars as a baseball player. He started pitching for the Los Angeles Dodgers in 1981. Valenzuela, José Canseco, and Ruben Sierra are just a few of the many Hispanics who have done very well in professional baseball. Roberto Clemente was an awesome baseball player. He is well known for taking care of people, too. He died in a plane crash carrying food and supplies to earthquake victims in 1972.

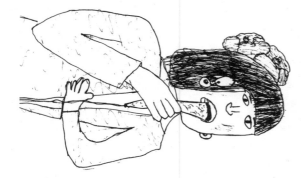

Nancy Lopez is well known for being one of the world's coolest female golfers. Lee Trevino and Chi Chi Rodriguez have been world-class golfers for many years.

Some Hispanics who have won gold medals in the Olympics are Arlene Limas (tae kwon do, which is a martial art), Tino Martinez (baseball), and Robin Ventura (baseball). Michael Carbajal won a silver medal in the 1988 Olympics and became a world boxing champion. Joe Vigil became an Olympic track coach. You can find more information on Hispanic athletes in books, magazines, and sports collector cards.

There are many Hispanics who are successful entertainers. Ruben Blades is an actor and a musician. Gloria Estefan is a singer. Los Lobos is a rock group. Rita Moreno, Edward James Olmos, and Jimmy Smits are actors. Geraldo Rivera has his own talk show. These are just a few Hispanic entertainers. There are many, many more.

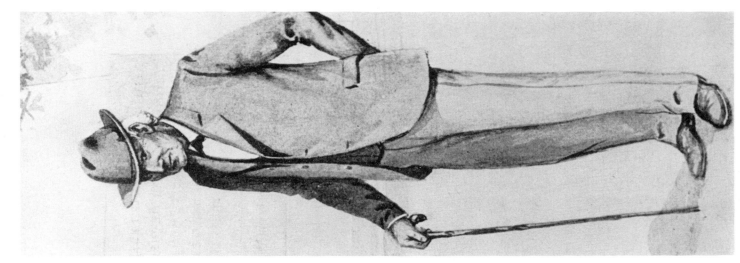

Diego Archuleta

OUR FAMOUS RELATIVES

Out of the eighty-two authors who participated in our writing workshop, three of us had famous relatives. One was Diego Archuleta, born in 1813. Another was Casmiro Barela, who was born in 1847. The last relative in our "Hall of Fame" is Rudolfo "Corky" Gonzales, who is still living today. We hope you enjoy reading about our relatives and finding out why they are famous.

Diego Archuleta
by Michael Laydon

It just so happened that my great-great-great-grandfather, Diego Archuleta, was involved in the fight over the Texas territory and the Alamo. Diego Archuleta was 22 years old when the Mexicans won the battle of the Alamo in 1835. Later, Diego was assigned a group of soldiers and was given the rank of lieutenant colonel of the militia by the Mexican government.

In 1841, when Mexico was invaded by the Texas–Santa Fe Expedition, Archuleta was in command of the troops that assisted in the capture of the Texans. In 1843, he was elected deputy of the National Mexican Congress of New Mexico. He received the Golden Cross Award for guarding the Mexican territory.

Archuleta was appointed second in command of the Mexican military. A few years later, he wanted to fight, but he knew it was a no-win situation against the increasing numbers of Anglos moving to the area. When my great-great-great-great-grandfather died, the funeral held for him

Casimiro Barela
by James Barela

Casimiro Barela

My great-great-great-uncle, Casimiro Barela, has been featured in a couple of biography books written by kids. He was born on May 4, 1847, in Embudo, New Mexico. His father, José, had pushed him to work hard so he would be successful in life. It looks like this advice paid off because Barela became a very famous person.

Barela helped write the Constitution of Colorado. He helped to make laws that benefited and protected Hispanics. He also served for forty years as a state senator of Colorado. Senator Barela spent over half of his life as a senator! He even had a town named after him, Barela, in southern Colorado. There is a stained glass window of

Senator Barela in the Colorado State Capitol. If you're ever in Denver, check it out. Casimiro Barela is a neat man to have as a great-great-great-uncle.

was the biggest ever in Santa Fe, New Mexico. Anyone would be very proud to have someone this important in their family tree!

Rudolfo ("Corky") Gonzalez
by Sergio Gonzalez

Another man who was a leader for the Hispanic movement was Rudolfo Gonzalez. He wrote a book called *I Am Joaquin (Yo Soy Joaquin)* and started a "Crusade for Justice" group to improve the pride of Hispanics. He was a leader in the Chicano movement. Because he is my grandfather, he will be called "Gramps" in the rest of this article.

Rudolfo "Corky" Gonzalez

Gramps came to our writing class for this book and spoke about many things. He told us that it is important to know where we come from so we can know who we are. It is important to learn our culture. We can learn about our culture from our family, on our own, or from books. But we have to know who our great-great-grandfathers were or else we cannot know who we really are and what our culture is.

Gramps said, "We can all be different, but we have the same father, God. We are all one, and we can still be friends, because we are all on the same earth. People don't have to take what they don't really need from someone else. Just taking over a whole group of people is wrong because they aren't like play toys. They are real people."

Gramps also told us that books are an important way for us to learn, because if we don't know something, then they can tell us. They can tell us about our culture or about anything we want to know. To

get books, Gramps worked for "Uncle Bob," who was not a relative, just a special person. In "Uncle Bob's" pawn shop, there was a big shelf of books about Hispanics and other groups. Gramps couldn't find these kinds of books in other places. He learned a lot from books and believes that they are very important and are to be treasured.

Gramps told all of the young authors that we were making his dream come true by writing a book about Hispanics.

Note to Readers: This is a very brief look at the Hispanic history of America. There are many versions of history, and we have chosen to give you just one short version. To get a more complete picture, you would need to research several sources and read much, much more.

FUN, FOOD, AND FESTIVALS

There are fiestas here.
There are recipes, too.
Fun, food, and festivals,
They are all for you.

FESTIVALS

Festivals are a special time for bringing the family together.

This part of our book touches on some religious and nonreligious celebrations. These Hispanic holidays are full of laughter and tears. Many Hispanics have adopted American customs into their holidays. For example, some Hispanic families now include the Christmas tree and Santa Claus as part of their Christmas traditions as well as Las Posadas and luminarias. Think about Hispanic customs you see in America as you read about Las Posadas, the Day of the Three Kings, Easter, Cinco de Mayo, and Day of the Dead.

Las Posadas

If you take part in Las Posadas, you probably will remember it until time ends. In most Spanish-speaking countries of the Americas, this special Christmas tradition begins on December 16. It is a Christmas play of Spanish heritage that began hundreds of years ago in southern Europe. This event brings to life how Joseph and Mary searched for a place for the Christ Child to be born. The word *posada* really means "inn" or "place of lodging." If you remember the story, Joseph and Mary could not find an inn where Mary could give birth, so they wandered until they found a stable with a manger.

frilly paper and filled with candy or trinkets. You can find out how to make a piñata in the art section of this book.

Many parts of Christmas in America have taken on Hispanic customs. All across our nation you will hear people say, "Feliz Navidad" (fay-LEES nah-vee-DAHD), which is Spanish for "Merry Christmas." It is not unusual for different kinds of churches and communities across our nation to celebrate Las Posadas by having real people dress up as Mary and Joseph and ride on a live donkey. Luminarias, containers or bags filled with lighted candles, are often used to decorate for Las Posadas or Christmas activities. In fact, Phoenix, Arizona, lights its Desert Botanical Garden with 6,000 luminarias for Christmas celebrations. Albuquerque, New Mexico, and San Antonio, Texas, are

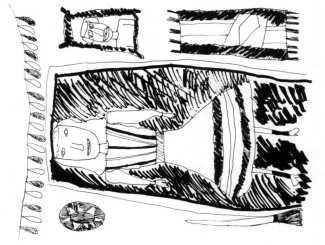

To celebrate the posada traditionally, people go from house to house and knock on the doors of friends and neighbors every night for nine days. They pretend to be searching for a place for Jesus to be born. They carry lanterns and small figures of Mary and Joseph. They create what is called a Nativity scene. They sing or recite poems wherever they go. It is sort of like caroling.

When they reach the house where the Nativity scene will be kept for the night, they have a big celebration. Some of the foods that people may have include tamales. They're made of pork or beef in a red chili-sauce dough, wrapped in a corn husk, and then steamed.

Las Posadas is celebrated by many Hispanic people, though the details may be different. For example, in Mexico, a posada party would have a piñata. A piñata is a clay pot or frame covered with only two of many American communities that schedule an annual Las Posadas celebration.

The Day of the Three Kings

Some people might think it is strange to have Christmas in January. On January 6, the Day of the Three Kings is celebrated. This special holiday comes exactly twelve days after the infant Jesus was born. This tradition comes from the Bible. According to the Bible, the Three Kings traveled twelve days to bring their gifts to the baby Jesus.

On the night of January 5, children leave their shoes or an empty shoe box stuffed with straw outside their house for the camels that the Three Kings ride. In the morning, the straw is gone, and in its place, they find candy, fruit, and toys. This tradition reminds the children of the Three Kings' journey to find the baby Jesus.

Some families might bake a festive kind of Hispanic bread to eat on this day. It is called Marzan bread. This holiday bread is shaped like a crown and has cherries and pineapple on it to represent jewels. It reminds the people of the crowns worn by the Three Kings. The baker puts a special surprise in the bread. It might be a small china doll, a charm, a coin, or even a ring. It is said that this special surprise will bring the person who finds it good luck.

In some places in Europe, the Day of the Three Kings is called Little Christmas.

Maybe they called it "Little Christmas" because they received little presents.

Many different churches celebrate the Day of the Three Kings in America. They call it Epiphany. We think a popular American Christmas song, "The Twelve Days of Christmas," might be related to this special day.

Easter Season

Easter is a religious holiday celebrated not only by Hispanics but by Christians all over our nation. Easter is the last day of a special season called Lent which lasts for forty days and nights before Easter Sunday.

The last week of Lent is called "Holy Week." Many churches celebrate at least three special days. Holy Thursday is first.

This is when Jesus met with his disciples, the twelve men that worked with him, and ate dinner with them for the last time. The dinner is referred to as the "Last Supper," and there are many famous paintings about this. Good Friday follows Holy Thursday. It is the Friday before Easter and is when Jesus was nailed to the cross. Finally, on Sunday, Easter is celebrated. The reason Christians celebrate this holiday is because this is a reminder of when Jesus rose from the dead. This holiday is in the spring when new life is beginning all around.

On Easter Sunday, many people wake up and go to church. After church, children go home to hunt for Easter eggs. Easter eggs are brightly decorated eggs that are hard boiled or plastic eggs with candy inside. Also during this day, family members gather together for a big dinner. Many Hispanic people celebrate like this all over the world.

Traditionally Hispanics celebrate holidays in a big way. Some Hispanics have special Easter eggs that are called *cascarones* (kahs-kah-RO-nays). These neat eggs might be fun for your family to make. They are whole eggshells filled with colored confetti. Children like to act as if they are in battles when they throw the eggs back and forth and sneak up on a friend and break the cascarone on his or her head.

Here are the directions for making cascarones. Make a hole about the size of a dime in one end to drain the raw insides. You can either drink the eggs in eggnog or fry them; just don't waste them. (Remember, Hispanics try to use everything they can.) Now clean the eggshell out by washing it. Let it dry. Start saving eggshells for about three months until Easter. When Easter is close you can make confetti out of recycled paper and fill half of the eggshell with this colored paper. Now you make a paste with flour and water to cover up the hole.

Cinco de Mayo

Cinco de Mayo (Fifth of May) is an exciting festival. This celebration takes place in many American cities across our nation as well as in Mexico. This has become a day for Mexican-Americans to share their traditions with many friends of different heritages.

The history behind this day goes back to 1862, when Napoleon III was the leader of France. Mexico owed large sums of money to France. Napoleon used this as an excuse to have his soldiers invade Mexico. There was a fierce battle called the Battle of Puebla. The fancy French army had many weapons and were well trained before the battle. Puebla was a small town south of Mexico City, with many farmers. The villagers had to make their own army with very few guns and bullets. The Mexicans were ragged and poor, but they fought on until the French left. We really were impressed by the courage of the Mexicans. This battle showed us that if you don't give up, you can win even if the odds are against you.

If you went to a Cinco de Mayo celebration in America you might hear a

mariachi band playing lively music and see beautiful dancers spinning. Street vendors would be selling colorful Mexican crafts. You might hear someone calling, "Tacos, burritos, enchiladas, and nachos!" You would smell delicious scents in the air and feel the excitement everywhere. In the month of May, try to locate a Cinco de Mayo celebration in your community so you can celebrate, too!

The Day of the Dead

So many Hispanic customs have their beginnings in completely different cultures. This holiday is a good example. Many native groups that lived in the New World had customs that showed respect for the dead. The Spanish also brought their own customs with them when they came to the New World. They have combined their traditions and call the celebration the Day of the Dead. It is not weird or scary. It is fun. It is a way for people to show respect for their dead relatives.

Some ideas behind this holiday come from many ancient groups of Indians. For example, the Taíno Indians of Cuba believed that at night their dead family members came back to their huts looking for food. Each night they would set out offerings of their favorite food for the relatives.

The Spanish explorers had a similar tradition they brought from their homeland. They had a special day they set aside to pray for people who had died. This day is November 1. It is called All Saints' Day. It is a way to show respect for the dead. The day after this has been named All

Souls' Day. It is a day when people pray for souls who have not found a resting place. These ideas of paying respect to the dead were blended together and became the Day of the Dead.

The Day of the Dead was originally celebrated over three days. On the first day, the living relatives would go to their dead relatives' graves and set out lots of candles and incense. They would also put marigolds on the graves because these flowers have a strong smell. The relatives hoped that the dead could find their way home by following the smells of the flowers, incense, and candles. At home, they spent the day preparing all the food that the dead person loved. They would put the food on a table, and no one could eat it until the dead person was given enough time to have some.

On the second day, the families would have big celebrations at their houses. They served more of the dead person's favorite foods. Pictures, a favorite dress, or even objects that belonged to that person were set out to remind people that these dead relatives were present. They would eat candies shaped like skeletons and coffins. The skeleton is a very important symbol for this celebration because it is the last thing that is left on the earth from their dead relatives. Relatives and friends danced and sang and spent a lot of time remembering their dead loved ones.

On the third day, the celebration became more widespread. There would be parades with floats and bands. Coffins were carried which had people in them dressed to look like skeletons. These skeletons moved just their arms and then their shoulders, slowly coming out of the coffin, as if to join the party.

Americans all across our country celebrate some aspects of this three-day celebration. Halloween is one example of

this. Halloween actually means "hallowed evening" or "holy eve." Many costumes include skeletons and skulls. This is often celebrated with festive foods and parties. Some Christian religions have a special church service to remember their dead. Other Americans might visit cemeteries or grave sites and leave flowers and flags on their graves to show love and respect for the dead.

FOOD

Hispanic cooking combines products and methods of two worlds. Remember when the Spanish invaders came to the New World, they brought livestock, cheeses, orchard fruits, and wheat along with their own ways of cooking. They met the different native groups such as the Maya of Mexico or the Taino Indians of Puerto Rico. We believe some Spanish explorers forced the natives to be their servants and made them start to use some Spanish ways in their cooking. These two heritages blended together, and a new way of cooking came about.

Let's think about how this could happen. For example, if your dad was cooking a recipe for your family, he might change it a little because he couldn't find one of the items in the recipe. Everyone might really like the new way he cooked the food, and now he has started a new recipe. This is one of the reasons Hispanic recipes for the same dish can be so different.

In discussing Hispanic food, we

Tortillas

found out that all eighty-two authors in our writing program had eaten in a Hispanic restaurant. We had all had tacos and burritos served in our school cafeteria. We were all familiar with many foods such as guacamole, enchiladas, salsa, and nachos. We made and tasted many Hispanic dishes. Below we have given recipes for the ones we liked and we think other kids can make. Ask your dad or mom if you can prepare some of our dishes. Read on to find recipes for drinks, appetizers, main dishes, and fruit popsicles.

A tortilla is a flat bread made from flour or corn. It can be stacked, rolled, folded, eaten alone, or eaten with many other things. You can buy machine-made tortillas in almost any American supermarket. We thought you might like to know how to make homemade ones. Here goes!

4½ cups flour
1 teaspoon salt or to taste
3 heaping tablespoons solid vegetable shortening
½ cup lukewarm water

Put flour in a big glass bowl. Then add salt and the vegetable shortening. Mix ingredients until the mixture looks like a rough rock. Add water slowly, and knead until the dough looks like a big ball. Cover with a towel and set aside for half an hour.

To make the tortillas, pinch out little balls of dough and put them on a cutting board that has lightly sprinkled flour on it. Then get a rolling pin and one ball of dough and roll it into a flat circle. Next get the flat circles and put them on a warm griddle. You have to cook each side until it's golden brown. Now you have great flour tortillas.

How to Fold a Tortilla for a Burrito

A burrito is a folded flour tortilla with different kinds of fixings in the middle such as cheese, meat, vegetables, and salsa. Have you ever noticed that at Mexican restaurants, they fold their burritos in a fancy way? Well, here we're going to teach you to do just that.

1. Place your meat and vegetables in a strip down the middle of your tortilla.
2. Fold the bottom part of the tortilla over your filling (just enough so you can still see some of the meat).
3. Fold in the sides.
4. Fold the top part over.
5. Now you can eat your meal with a fork or with your hands.

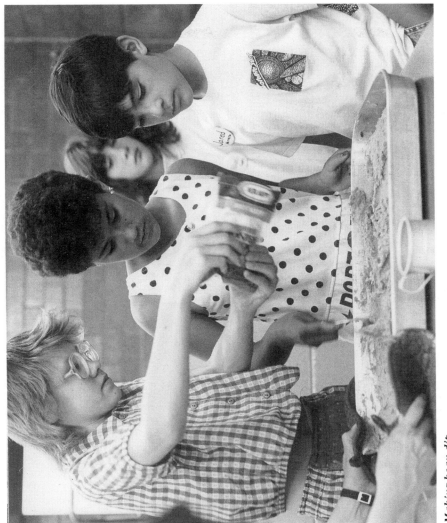

Making bean dip

Salsa para los Niños (Dip for Children)

Tired of the plain old salsa? If you are, then why don't you try the following recipe? Those of you who don't know what salsa is, listen carefully. Salsa is a thick tomatoey sauce that can either be spicy or mild. Here's a recipe we liked. (It makes 3 cups.)

1 28-ounce can Italian-style tomatoes
¼ cup onions
½ tablespoon vinegar
1 tablespoon salad oil
1 teaspoon finely crushed oregano leaves
1 teaspoon finely crushed parsley leaves

Crush tomatoes by hand. Add the rest of the ingredients. This salsa is a mild sauce that most children like. You should put it in a light-colored bowl so people will know it's mild.

This salsa is wonderful on tacos, burritos, nachos, corn chips, and most Mexican dishes. It's guaranteed to be a favorite at parties.

Guacamole

3 large peeled avocados
½ cup chopped onion
1 cup chopped tomato
1 tablespoon lime juice

First cut up the avocados and put them in a pan or bowl. Save the seed in the middle for decoration when done. Then take the tomatoes and onions and spread them around the avocados. Mash all the ingredients together. After mashing the avocados, put the lime juice into the mixture and mix it one last time.

HINT: Place the seed in the finished dip to keep it from turning brown.

Huevos Rancheros

You need a frying pan and a stove to make this. Ingredients are eggs, oil, tortillas, and salsa. Put the frying pan on the stove and warm the oil in the frying pan. Get some eggs and crack them into the frying pan. Now fry the eggs. Put a tortilla on a plate, then put the eggs on the tortilla. Take some salsa and put it on top of the eggs. Roll your tortilla over everything. Then eat it up!

Chorizo con Huevos (Scrambled Eggs and Mexican Sausage)

8 eggs
3-4 links chorizo sausage
Garlic powder

First peel off the skin of the chorizo. Next get a frying pan and mash the chorizo in the pan with a big spoon. Cook the chorizo with a little bit of nonstick oil. When done, drain all of the chorizo grease. Next put the eggs in the pan. Scramble the eggs. Mix the eggs, chorizo, and the amount of garlic powder wanted. Serve with a flour tortilla.

Chicken Enchiladas

1 chicken, about 3 pounds
1 medium onion, chopped
3 tablespoons butter
1 can cream of chicken soup
1 can cream of mushroom soup
1 cup chicken broth.
1 4-ounce can green chiles, chopped
1 dozen Candy's corn tortillas (or other brand)
1 pound longhorn cheese, shredded

Cook and bone chicken. Brown onion in butter. Add soups, broth, chiles, and chicken, and heat well. In a 9″ × 13″ pan, layer the tortillas, chicken sauce, and cheese. Repeat until the casserole is filled, ending with cheese. Bake 30 minutes at 350 degrees. Serves eight.

Arrachera al Carbon (Mexican Fajitas)

1 pound trimmed skirt steak, cut into 3-inch lengths

1 onion per pound grilled with meat

1 green pepper per pound grilled with meat

1 lime per pound grilled with meat

Salt and pepper to taste

Squeeze lime juice over the meat. Grill on a charcoal grill. Serve with guacamole, Candy's tortillas, and lots of salsa. Serves four.

Atole de Fresa (Creamy Strawberry Breakfast Drink)

This drink is very smooth. It goes well with breakfast or on a cold day. This drink would be very enjoyable after sledding instead of hot chocolate!

2 quarts fresh or frozen strawberries

½ cup white corn meal substitute

½ cup all-purpose cream of wheat or wheat flour

4 cups milk, scalded

2 cups water

1 cup sugar

1 teaspoon vanilla

A few drops red food coloring

½ teaspoon cinnamon

Squash the well-washed strawberries. Blend the white corn meal with the water. Slowly add the sugar and stir for ten minutes. The mixture should be thick. Add the strawberries, vanilla, cinnamon, cream, and the few drops of food coloring. Heat until boiling begins, stirring every few minutes. Serve in mugs or cups. Makes four quarts.

Chocolate Mexicano (Mexican Hot Chocolate)

When it's cold outside and you need something warm to drink, why don't you try this?

2 3-ounce cakes or tablets Mexican chocolate

(6 oz. sweet cooking chocolate can be used instead)

6 cups milk

2 teaspoons cinnamon (only if using cooking chocolate)

2 teaspoons sugar (if you want)

Combine all the ingredients in a saucepan and cook over low heat. Stir constantly until the chocolate has melted and the mixture is blended. Just before serving, use an egg beater and beat until smooth. Serves four.

Fruit Punch

This fruit punch is a delicious drink on a hot summer day.

¼ cup sugar
1 cup orange juice
4 cups grape juice
½ lemon, sliced
½ orange, sliced
1 small apple or peach, cut into thin wedges
4 cups club soda
Ice

Put the sugar, orange juice, and grape juice in a pitcher. Add the lemon, orange, and apple or peach slices. Stir the mixture until the sugar disappears. Just before you serve the drink, put in the club soda. Put in ice if you want to and you have a delicious drink.

Paletas
(Fruit Popsicles)

2 cups sweet pureed fruit
1 cup juice
2 heaping tablespoons sugar
½ teaspoon lime juice

Get the fruit you like and mash it. Then put it into a bowl. Add the fruit juice and mix together. Then add the sugar and lime juice to keep the color of the fruit. Put contents into two ice cube trays. Stick toothpicks into the center of each cube. Freeze for 3 to 7 hours. Then you have a cold treat.

DANCES

What would a festival be without dancing? Dancing is done all over the world. All cultures have some form of the art of dance. In fact, many anthropologists, people who study cultures, believe dance actually started when male animals wanted to attract female animals. They jumped around and looked beautiful so that the female animal would notice them. A lot of dances are about this type of boy or girl thing. Dance was used in many cultures to ask the gods for favors. One example of this was a dance done to ask the gods for rain. In some cultures, only men dance,

ican folkloric dancing began. This type of dance is very important to the Hispanics because it expresses emotion and heritage. It is a blend of the Spanish, Indian, and Caribbean cultures. Folk dancing is handed down from one generation to the next. Many folk dances were made for pleasure. Some of these dances are for dating and have the dancers flirt with each other. The Cuban rumba is a dance that tells the story of a flirtatious exchange. The dancers move to show boy meets girl, boy chases girl, and girl runs away! In a dance called Bullfighting, the matador is flirting with death.

The styles of costumes for the dances have been passed down from generation to generation. For example, Mexican costumes are chosen by color and expression for each dance and are handmade. The dancers like to pick the colors for their costumes unless they are for a group per-

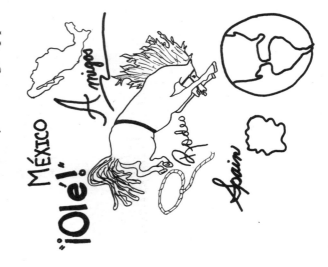

while in others, only women dance. In the Hispanic culture, both men and women dance.

Dancing has many basic elements such as steps, gestures, rhythm, and techniques. Dancing is made up of parts of people's movements like walking, jumping, skipping, running, hopping, galloping, sliding, swaying, and turning. In ancient times, the dancer made his own music by singing, shouting, or clapping. As dances became more involved, musicians started to provide the music. Specific music was selected to go with certain dances. The basic rhythm of a dance is very closely related to the music. Music and dance belong together. They are both based on rhythm and movement.

Dance can be an expression of our emotions, or it can help us feel a specific way. Dance has helped some religious people express their love for God. Dance can also be used to tell a story.

In the early 1800s, traditional Mex-

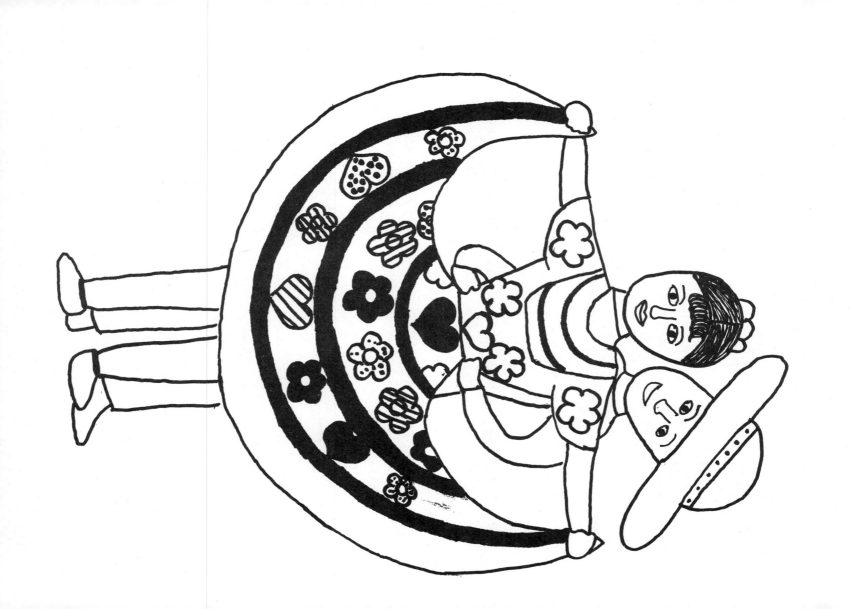

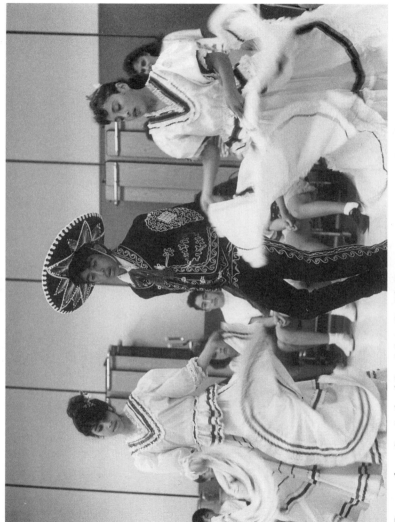

Dancers from Our Lady of Guadalupe Parish, Denver

formance in which all the costumes must match. The dresses usually have full skirts with lots of ruffles, lace, and ribbons. They are very long, almost to the ground, and make the girls look like big butterflies when they hold their dresses out to their sides. The men usually wear black suits with white shirts. The pant legs are tapered with rows of silver buttons down the outside of the leg. A large sombrero, a wide brimmed hat, is the finishing touch on the men's costume. Some dancers use colorful fluttering scarfs, castanets, and hand clapping.

The dance called La Raspa, meaning to scrape or scratch, is a Mexican folk dance consisting of an alternate shuffling of the feet forward and backward and ending with a polka pivot. This dance has specific music for its dance steps. Children dance La Raspa at parties and birthdays and just to feel good.

The Mexican Hat Dance (Jarabé Tapatío) is a well-known Mexican dance. This dance came together when popular Spanish music was put with musical styles of blacks and Indians. The Jarabé became known as the Mexican Hat Dance because it's a dance performed around a hat. The boy dancer dances on one side of the hat, and the girl dancer dances on the other side. It's sort of a boyfriend and girlfriend

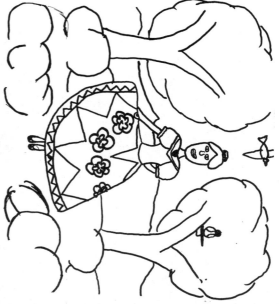

type of dance because all the time the dancers are dancing they are flirting with each other. The Jarabé Tapatío has con-tinued to be a popular Mexican dance. It's frequently performed by the Ballet Folklorico Nacional across America. Many Hispanic communities across our country have Ballet Folklorico dance groups such as the ones in San Antonio, Texas, and Los Angeles, California.

Today in America, strolling musical groups called mariachis perform at street fairs and in restaurants. The mariachi groups have singers, musicians, and dancers. The dancers perform to lively music. They use a few basic steps, like hopping, heel and toe tapping, and scratching. The musicians use all types of guitars, brass horns (like trumpets), and percussion instruments like maracas and castanets.

Hispanic dancing is a world filled with history and tradition. It is a really good thing for kids to learn. Throughout America, in community churches and centers, there are many groups that hold classes to learn Hispanic dance. If you are interested in being a member of a dance group, contact Hispanic churches and centers to ask them about opportunities in your area. After students learn to dance, some perform for festivals and other celebrations. Learning Hispanic dance is a great way to learn about the culture while having lots of fun!

Note to Readers: There are so many more Hispanic festivals, recipes, and customs to explore. We hope you take the time to attend a Hispanic celebration or do some investigation on your own.

ART

Art has a great part in history.
It brings to beauty life's mystery.
The paint, the pen, the ordinary thing.
The joy and pain that art can bring.

As Americans across our country become more aware of taking care of our environment, American artists are starting to use recycled items in their art. This trend has been a part of Hispanic art for years. Many Hispanic artists use creativity to turn ordinary household stuff into beautiful, interesting pieces of art.

The artists discussed below create their art using Hispanic techniques, and at the same time, they portray their Hispanic heritage. Hispanics have come from Cuba, Mexico, Spain, Puerto Rico, and many other places around the world. Where they come from makes their art different; for example, Cubans, who are islanders, might paint water, but Mexicans might paint mountains or land because they have lived near this type of area. Religion is an important part of Hispanic tradition, and it is this religious heritage that is used in Hispanic art. Artists use their feelings about family, saints, and Hispanic tradition to help learn and share the beauty of the Hispanic culture.

Also in this chapter we will tell about folk art, *retablos* and *santos*. Many times, saints and other religious beliefs are used as ideas for this art, and so are things from everyday life. Some of the art is colorful, and some is plain, but all of it is a beautiful expression of the artist's talents.

Piñatas, luminarias, and *molas* are three exciting art projects we talk about which you will be able to make. We have

She used plain old ordinary ballpoint pens in red, blue, black, green, and purple, but not all of her drawings had color in them. Chelo enjoyed painting but not as much as she enjoyed drawing. She called her drawing "Filigree Art, a new Texas culture." She took a three-dimensional design and turned it into a flat drawing. Most of her art ideas came from the things she learned and saw at church because she didn't go to school.

Writing poetry was another of Chelo's interests. She has won prizes for her poetry. Sometimes she would have poetry in her drawings, using plain words to express her ideas.

Even though Chelo's family didn't always encourage her, she always knew she wanted to be an artist. Her designs and details amaze many of her admirers.

Carmen Lomas Garza

Carmen Lomas Garza is a talented artist who has shared her Hispanic heritage in her work. She was born in Kingsville, Texas, in 1948. Garza was the second child born in a family with five children. She went to a public school in Kingsville, and

provided the directions and a list of materials for each at the end of this chapter.

Read on to find out about five Hispanic artists, three types of Hispanic art, and three art projects that you might like to make at home.

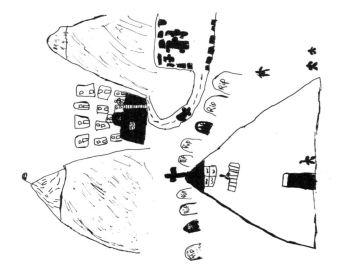

ARTISTS

Consuelo Gonzalez Amezcua

Do you know which Hispanic artist's nickname was Chelo? It was Consuelo Gonzalez Amezcua. She was born in Mexico in 1903 but was brought up in Del Rio, Texas. She was offered a scholarship to attend an art school but wasn't able to attend because of her father's death. She never really went to school to learn art.

Chelo began drawing with doodling.

one thing she remembered from her childhood was getting spanked for speaking Spanish in class. Speaking Spanish in school was against the law then. Garza graduated from the Texas Arts and Industries University in 1972.

Garza's mother was a florist, and her grandmother made paper flowers. Their artistic talent and projects helped Garza to decide, when she was a teenager, to become an artist.

In college, Garza became involved in "El Movimiento," the Chicano movement. Artists like Garza joined this movement because they were proud to be of Mexican descent. Their paintings showed a special pride in their heritage. A historian of the Chicano movement, Jacinto Quirarte, has stated that the reason these artists enjoyed their work was not to be famous but "to teach the Chicano community about itself, to strengthen it, and to nurture it." This means to learn more about yourself and to be proud of who you are. Garza wanted to help the community grow in its understanding of its heritage.

Garza's paintings sometimes show Hispanic people with their family. For example, one of her paintings, called *Sandia Watermelon*, shows a scene where the parents, children, and grandparents are together on the porch eating watermelon. Extended families living together such as grandparents, aunts, uncles, grandchildren, and cousins are important in the Hispanic culture. Another one of her famous pictures done in 1977 is called *Death Cart*. This picture shows a skeleton that could represent a part of the November 1

Day of the Dead celebration. (Read more about the Day of the Dead in Fun, Food, and Festivals.)

Another example of Garza's work is her *Homage to Frida Kahlo*, a famous Mexican artist who is an inspiration to many Mexican-American women artists. Kahlo's paintings are like little memories from life, a life that had a strong desire to paint even with pain and suffering.

Carmen Lomas Garza now lives in San Francisco, California, and has had exhibits at the San Francisco Museum of Modern Art, the Mexican Museum of San Francisco, El Museo del Barrio (Museum of the Barrio) of New York, and Intar Latin American Gallery of New York. Garza was recently featured in *Hispanic Art in the United States: Thirty Contemporary Painters and Sculptors* by John Beardsley and Jane Livingston. You might ask for this book at your library so you can see some photographs and examples of her work.

Eduardo Chavez

Eduardo Chavez was an interesting man. He was born in Wagon Mound, New Mexico, in 1917. Even though he went to Colorado Springs Fine Arts Center for a short time, he believes he taught himself to paint. Señor Chavez featured American subjects in his murals, which are located in Glenwood Springs and Denver, Colorado; Geneva, Nebraska; Center, Texas; and Fort Warren, Wyoming. He has traveled throughout Europe and Mexico.

When Señor Chavez started his art career, he had two really good friends who one day died in a car accident. After his friends died, he made all blue paintings because painters paint the things they feel. He used blue because it represents sad feelings. As time passed, Chavez started to add more color to his paintings. Soon his paintings were more colorful and less sad. Today, his blue paintings are his most famous works of art. Our favorite painting of his is *Ocate 1*. It's very colorful. It has many shades of blue, and the colors seem to dance around all the other colors. This is a happy blue painting!

Octavio Medellin

Octavio Medellin is a Hispanic sculptor who is well known throughout Texas. He uses wood and stone to sculpt his wonderful statues and sculptures. He usually sculpts figures and animals that look strong and sturdy. They are huge and very heavy.

Medellin was born in Mexico in 1907. Living during the Mexican Revolution was not easy, and his family was forced to move many times. Finally they settled in San Antonio, Texas, in 1920. That is when he began to study art. He studied Indian crafts, which had a great influence on his sculptures. He also studied painting and life drawing. He tried to enroll in the San Carlos Academy of Mexico but was not accepted because he didn't have enough schooling in art. He began sculpting in 1933. No one had ever taught him how to sculpt, so he is considered to be self-taught.

Medellin set up his very own gallery, the Villita, to help himself and other artists sell their artwork. After starting the art gallery, he taught for three years at two museums. It seems that you have to sell your art before anyone thinks you know enough to tell others about it. Sometime later, Syracuse University Library asked for his papers and art studies to put in its Collection of Manuscripts of Sculptors. After that, he began to run his own art school.

A lot of his sculptures have themes about history. One of Medellin's pieces is a great example of this living history. It is called *The History of Mexico*. On each side of it are carvings of things that happened at a certain time. These carvings tell a story to the viewer.

Since the late thirties, Medellin's art has been exhibited a lot, and he continues to make lifelike sculptures. He is a great sculptor because he uses ideas from his own mind and puts them into his pieces of art.

Gregorio Marzan

Gregorio Marzan was born in 1906 in Puerto Rico. He attended school until he was nine years old, when he had to find a job. Marzan worked on the island of Puerto Rico as a carpenter and as a field hand. While he was working there, he got married and had five children. In 1937, he decided to move to New York City so he could find a better job. New York had many more job opportunities to help support his family. Sadly, his wife died before he got to New York. Eventually, when he could afford it, he brought his five kids,

who had been living with their grand-mother, to New York.

In New York, Marzan couldn't find a job as a carpenter, but he did find a job making toys, dolls, and stuffed animals. He worked in lots of toy factories until he retired in 1971.

During his retirement, Marzan started making small birds and houses typical of rural Puerto Rico to sell to gift shops. He tried to sell these home decorations to several gift shops, but they were not interested. When he was trying to sell his work to the gift shop at El Museo del Barrio, the museum director thought that his pieces were so good that they belonged in the museum! This happened in 1979. The museum has been collecting his art pieces ever since.

Marzan does not think of himself as an artist. He says he can make anything that he sees. His ideas come to him when he is walking around or they come from his memories of Puerto Rico. We consider him an artist and like his work because it is very beautiful. For example, *The Dachs-bund* has a lot of glitter and parts of it look like shiny colored ribbon.

SOME TRADITIONAL HISPANIC ART FORMS

Retablos

Retablos (re-TAH-blohs) are small, reli-gious oil paintings. These paintings help others to see a picture of what a holy per-son might look like such as Jesus or the

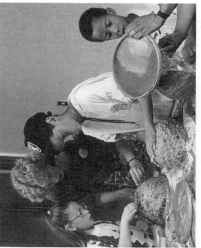

Making recycled paper baskets

Lady of Guadalupe, who is also called the Virgin Mary. They are usually painted on tin by untrained artists who haven't gone to an art school. Some artists use copper instead of tin for the retablos. Retablos were a favorite form of art in the early years of the nineteenth century. Thou-sands of these holy pictures were painted during that time.

Santos

Later, some artists decided to carve saints and holy people out of wood instead of painting them on tin and copper. These works are called *santos*. They are three-dimensional so you can walk around them. They are colorful, with reds, yel-lows, blues, greens, and browns. Black was used for outlines. Santos can be sev-eral inches or a few feet in height. They are very beautiful.

Folk Art

Artists also did folk art. Much of this was like the santos, only plain, with no colors

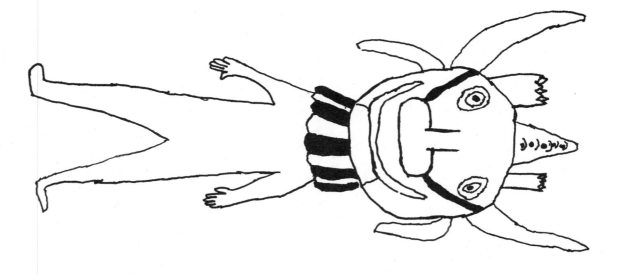

...at all! We saw some that were three-dimensional. Folk art makes statements about things in the everyday lives of the Hispanic people. These events could include work, gardening, sports, or church or family activities. For Hispanic people, folk art is an expression of the way they carry out everyday activities. It paints a better picture of their community.

Folk art changed a little from the colorful santos but not very much. The folk artists wanted something new and different. They had less color compared to the retablos and the santos. Santos looked more realistic than the retablo paintings. The folk art is plainer and doesn't have as many details. Folk art is usually made of natural wood so there is only the color of the wood.

The Hispanic people often use things like old cardboard and paper to write or draw on or even to make into new paper. They also use pieces of tin and copper and other materials to create sculptures. They use these leftover scraps to create interesting pieces of art. Something like an aluminum can could be made into a colorful Christmas tree decoration.

Folk Art Projects

Piñatas

Making piñatas is an experience filled with history. Piñatas didn't start in Mexico. They started in Italy, and they were first called *pignattas*. Back in the European Renaissance of the fourteenth and fifteenth centuries, the pignattas were shaped like a clay ice cream cone. This cone shape was called a *pigna*. Later the single cone became three cones put together like a star. The star symbolized the Three Kings and the gifts they brought to baby Jesus at Christmas. Each point represents one of those Three Kings.

In 1498, on Columbus's third voyage,

Making piñatas

Father de Las Casas, a Spanish priest, traveled as a missionary to Cuba. He showed the piñatas to the native people and told them how each point represented a king. Father de Las Casas saw how excited the natives were to find treasures and candies in the points of the star piñatas. He told them that if they became Christians, the Three Kings would fill the piñatas with candy and toys for them. The Indians, thinking this was true and knowing how much they loved the candy and goodies, decided to accept some of the Christian beliefs.

Mexico first used piñatas during the Feast of the Three Kings. Young children were told that the Three Kings were the ones who put candy and toys in the piñatas. Children made their piñatas big because the bigger the star, the more gifts the kings would leave. At celebrations, they would hit the piñata with a stick. It would crack open, and the goodies would spill out.

Today, piñatas are a fun thing for any party. They are a smashing success, literally. You can make a piñata, too! Here's how.

Materials: You will need one balloon, some thin newspaper strips, art glue or regular glue for making papier-mâché, three large rectangular pieces of paper, string, masking tape, tissue paper, Elmer's Glue, and lots of clean-up supplies.

1. First blow up your balloon.
2. Take the newspaper strips and put them through the art glue that you put into a small tub.
3. Next, take your pointer finger and your middle finger, put them like scissors, and go down the strip. Be careful not to tear it. You do this so the art glue doesn't glob up and look sloppy.
4. Now wrap your balloon with the glued strips enough so that its color doesn't show through. Set your balloon to dry in the sun for about a day. Make sure it doesn't get dirty and that it does not drip on people.
5. Now you're ready to take the three rectangular pieces of paper and turn them into cones. You do this by hold-

ing the paper sideways with your thumb and pointer finger in the middle. Fold the paper toward the middle, being careful not to crease it. Do the same with the other side. Make sure there is a point at the top of the cone.

6. Do all of this with the three pieces of paper and tape the cone together so it doesn't unravel.

7. After that, tape these to the balloon so that it appears to be a three-pointed star when you look down on it.

8. Your next step is to take the three pieces of string and tie them together so they look like a fat Y. Now put the strings where they are tied together under the piñata. Bring them up in between the cones, and tie them together again at the top. Now you'll be able to hang up your piñata.

9. Then take the tissue paper and cut it into one- to two-inch strips, the length of the paper. Fold the strips in half and cut the width of the strip to make a fringe. Be careful to keep it attached.

10. Take the side that's not fringed and put a thin line of Elmer's Glue on it.

11. Take the piñata, and start wrapping the tissue paper you just fringed around the tip at one cone. Make sure you cover the newspaper. When you get to the center, wrap the strips in a circular motion, being careful to cover the top and bottom. If you missed a spot, you can use the extra tissue paper to patch it up.

12. If you want to, you can use any extra tissue paper as streamers. These are glued to the pointed ends of the piñata to make it more decorative.

13. Now you get to clean up! Let your piñata dry out by hanging it up somewhere for a while. This also makes your room look festive, and you can even have fun while you're cleaning!

Molas

Molas are a colorful part of Hispanic culture. Their origin goes back to the Cuña Indians of Panama. A mola is a brightly colored geometric design. The Indians

Molas are fun to make. In fact, many American tourists have brought these back from their visits to the Panama Canal area. Many art teachers in American schools have their students make molas as a Hispanic art project. They can be all sorts of colors and shapes, and you can start with any size you want.

This is a fun way of making molas.

Materials: Pencil, white paper, scissors, lots of colored construction paper, a large piece of white paper, and glue.

1.   Draw a picture of your design on the

used shapes of living things like plants and animals for their designs. A mola is made of layers of the colored design placed one on top of the other. The Cuña Indians used fabric for their layers. The shapes were just a bit bigger for each layer. They would put these layered shapes on a background and cover this background as much as possible. They could make them into pillows and blankets, and they even put the molas right on their clothes. The Indians still make molas today. If you like the molas on the Indians' clothing, they take them off and sell them to you.

Luminarias

Luminarias are lights set out along paths to lead the way on dark nights. During Las Posadas, which is a reenactment of when Joseph and Mary were looking for a place to stay, many people use luminarias to light the sidewalks and doorways to their homes. In America, luminarias are used to put on houses and walkways to light the way for guests. This is usually done around Christmas time because they are such a festive decoration.

There are many different kinds of luminarias. Sometimes they are made using a brown bag with a candle inside. The kind described here is made out of a

Making a mola

white paper. You have to make all of the designs out of something in nature.

2. Cut it out with your scissors and trace your shape onto a piece of construction paper. Every time you cut it out, trace your shape bigger than the last one, and use a different color.

3. Then layer them from the biggest on the bottom to the littlest one on top.

4. After that, glue each design together.

5. Glue all of the designs on one large piece of paper covering as much of the paper as possible.

Molas are a great way to show one thing the ancient Cuña people do. You can make one and hang it on the wall to show to your friends.

tin can, using a hammer and nail to put in holes for a neat lighted effect that shines through the spaces. The designs are flashed across the walls and ceiling where the luminarias sit.

Materials: Tin can, wood post, hammer, nails, can opener, paper, pencil, and imagination. The tin can could be any kind such as a coffee can, bean can, or soup can. It needs to be able to slip on the round wood post.

1. Use your pencil and paper to make a repeating design something like this.

2. Get a tin can (like a small coffee can). Cut the ends out of the can with a can opener.
3. Tape your designs onto the tin can.
4. Take the wood post and stick it through the ends of the can.
5. Put the end of the posts on two tables or two chairs.

6. Use the hammer and nails to put holes for each dot on the design. Remember to pound the nail through the tin so that when you put the candle in the can, the light will shine through.
7. When your design is done, remove the tape and paper design, put a candle inside, and place the luminaria in a dark place so that you can see how it works.

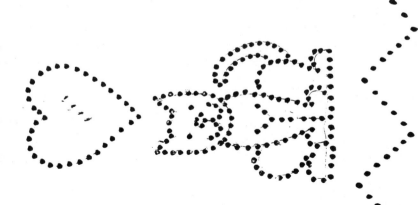

FUN WITH WORDS

Words! Words! Words!
Lots and lots of words.
Phrases, jokes, riddles, laughter.
Lots and lots of fun with words.

We would like you to see how neat words can be in English and Spanish. Both languages surround us in many areas of the United States. Fun with Words will help you to learn and understand *dichos* [DEE-chohs], *chistes* [CHEEH-stehs] or *bromas* [BROH-mahs], *adivinanzas* [ah-dee-vee-NAHN-sahs], cognates, *palabras* [pah-LAH-brahs], *frases* [FRAH-sehs], *números* [NOO-meh-rohs], *colores* [coh-LOH-rehs], and Spanish names.

DICHOS [Sayings]

Some dichos are passed on from generation to generation. They are sayings that you hear often. For example, "*Del dicho al hecho hay mucho trecho*" —It is easier said than done. You can't always translate dichos directly. Sometimes they help you learn lessons or convince you to do something. These sayings are like a piece of advice and will help you to avoid mistakes with people and in life. They will never grow old. Here are some dichos we picked out just for you.

"*Con la vara que midas, serás medido*" [With the rod that you measure, you will be measured].

"*Hablando del rey de Roma, mira quién se asoma*" [Speaking of the devil, look who's here].

"*El que no habla, dios no lo oye*" [If you don't speak up, you won't be heard].

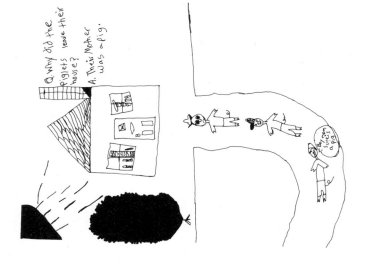

CHISTES [Jokes]

Chistes are jokes in question and answer form that make people laugh. They are also known as bromas. Some chistes are very strange. They are easier to understand in Spanish than in English. Sometimes it's hard to understand or catch the punch line. To help you understand chistes more, here are some.

Spanish

P: ¿Por qué tienen los elefantes la piel arrugada?

R: Porque no se lo quitan para dormir.

English

Q: Why do elephants have wrinkled skin?

A: Because they don't take it off to sleep.

Spanish

P: ¿Por qué no dejo Caperucita Roja que el lobo se la comiera?

R: Porque no tenía permiso de su mamá.

English

Q: Why did Little Red Riding Hood not let the wolf eat her?

A: Because she didn't have permission from her mom.

Spanish

P: ¿Por qué se fueron los cochinitos de su casa?

R: Porque su mamá era una cochina.

English

Q: Why did the piglets leave their house?

A: Because their mother was a pig.

Spanish

¿Sabes que le dijo un olvidadizo a otro?

¿Qué?

Ay, se me olvidó.

English

Do you know what one forgetful person said to another?

What?

Oops, I just forgot.

ADIVINANZAS [Riddles]

Adivinanzas are riddles. They are similar to jokes but longer. Sometimes they are confusing, funny, and mysterious. They use words that sound alike but have different meanings, and this makes them funny. These words are called puns. When you try to translate them from English to Spanish, they're not as funny. This is because

P: ¿Por que tienen los elefantes la piel arrugada?
R: Porque no se lo quitan para dormir.
Q: Why do elephants have wrinkled skin?
A: Because they don't take it off to sleep.

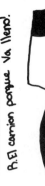

in English the similar words cannot be used to mean the same as in Spanish. If you know someone who speaks Spanish, try to get them to tell the adivinanzas because the humor is in the pronunciation. You have to use your mind to get the answer, but it's funny even if you don't get it. We think jokes make you laugh harder than riddles.

Spanish
Baila, pero no en la harina. ¿Qué es?

English
She dances, but not in the flour. What is she?

Respuesta/Answer: Bailarina [dancer]
This just combines the two words below.
(baila : dances) + (harina : flour)

Spanish
Una vieja larga y seca, que le escurre la manteca. ¿Qué es?

English
A tall old woman, dried up stick, who drips fat. Who is it?
Respuesta/Answer: Una vela [a candle]

Spanish
Blanco como la nieve,
Prieto como el carbón,
Anda y no tiene pies,
Habla y no tiene boca. ¿Qué es?

English
White as snow,
Black as coal,
It walks and has no feet,
It speaks and has no mouth. What is it?
Respuesta/Answer: Una carta (a letter)

COGNATES

We thought you might enjoy some cognates. Cognates are words in Spanish and English that sound the same and have similar spelling and the same meaning.

Now, it is with great pleasure that we proudly present some cognates we thought of just for you, just for fun. You might even find these elsewhere in our book.

English	Spanish	Pronunciation
Chocolate	*el chocolate*	[choh-coh-LAH-teh]
Tomato	*el tomate*	[toh-MAH-teh]
Boots	*las botas*	[BOH-tahs]
Lemon	*el limón*	[lee-MOHN]
Applaud	*aplaudir*	[ah-plah-oo-THEER]
Rose	*la rosa*	[ROH-sah]
Map	*el mapa*	[MAH-pah]
Paper	*el papel*	[pah-PEHL]
Music	*la música*	[MOO-see-cah]
Musician	*el músico*	[MOO-see-coh]
Bottle	*la botella*	[boh-TEH-yah]
Cafeteria	*la cafetería*	[cah-feh-teh-REE-yah]
Much	*mucho*	[MOO-choh]
Salad	*la ensalada*	[ehn-sah-LAH-dah]
Virgin	*la Virgin*	[BEER-hen]
Numbers	*los números*	[NEW-mehr-dohs]
Colors	*los colores*	[coh-LOH-rehs]
Vegetable	*el vegetal*	[veh-heh-TAHL]
Explorer	*el explorador*	[ehks-ploh-rah-DOHR]
Intelligent	*inteligente*	[een-teh-lee-HEHN-teh]
No	*no*	[noh]

SPANISH PLACE-NAMES

Have you ever wondered why so many places in the southeastern and southwestern United States have Spanish names? It is estimated that over 100,000 Spaniards came to the Western Hemisphere during the first half of the sixteenth century. When they came, they named many communities, rivers, areas, and settlements. Here are just a few for you to visit.

Arizona (Arid Zone)
Colorado (Colored State)
Florida (Place of Flowers)
Montana (Mountain)
Rio Grande (Big River)
El Paso (The Pass)
San Antonio (Saint Anthony)
San Jose (Saint Joseph)
Santa Fe (Saint Faith)
Pueblo (Small Town)
San Francisco (Saint Francis)
Los Angeles (The Angels)
San Diego (Saint James)
Trinidad (Trinity)

The next time you look at a map, try to see how many Spanish names you can find. A clue to look for is that many Spanish words end with a vowel. Spanish names for places often include: San (male saint), Santa (female saint), río (river), and the words Los or Las (the).

LOS COLORES [Colors]

Here is a poem describing colors. We translated each color into Spanish and placed it right next to the color word.

I see red (*rojo*) as the fire at night,
I see the sky as blue (*azul*) and white (*blanco*).
I see brown (*café*) in coffee cups,
I see black (*negro*) spots on little pups.
I see green (*verde*) as stubby grass,
I see gray (*gris*) as swimming bass.
I see gold (*oro*) as the burning sun,
I see silver (*plata*) as a shining gun.
I see orange (*anaranjado*) as pumpkin seeds,
I see yellow (*amarillo*) in dandelion weeds.
I see pink (*rosado*) as a tie-dyed ant,
I see purple (*morado*) as a frozen eggplant.
No matter what color it is that we seek,
It makes no difference what language we speak.

FRASES [Phrases]

Here is a list of phrases that are easy to learn. You may want to use some of them the next time you are talking to a Hispanic friend.

Or, it might be fun to fool a friend by learning to say these Spanish sayings and using them.

Good morning	*Buenos días*
Good evening	*Buenas tardes*
Goodnight	*Buenas noches*
Good grief	*Qué barbaridad*
See you tomorrow.	*Hasta mañana.*
Hello	*Hola*
Good-bye	*Adiós*
How are you?	*¿Cómo está usted?*
Clean your room.	*Limpia tu cuarto.*
Be quiet/Shut up!	*No hables/¡Cállate!*
Get lost.	*Vete/¡Quítate de aquí!*
I love you.	*Te amo.*
Kiss me.	*Bésame.*
Thank you.	*Gracias.*

Please.	*Por favor.*
Excuse me.	*Con permiso./ Perdóneme.*
You're welcome.	*De nada.*
What is your name?	*¿Cómo se llama?*
I'm lost.	*Estoy perdido.*
Can you help?	*¿Me pueda ayudar?*
I don't speak Spanish.	*No hablo español.*
I don't know.	*No se.*
Merry Christmas	*Feliz Navidad*
Happy New Year	*Prospero Año Nuevo*

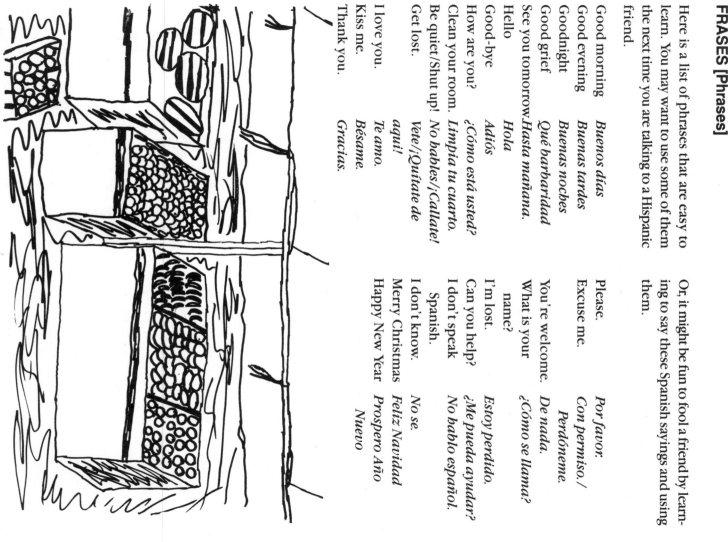

CUENTOS [Stories]

Stories are fun to hear:
Full of laughter and fear.
A word of wisdom to everyone.
A tradition of real Hispanic fun.

Storytelling is a very important part of the Hispanic culture. Before there was even a written language, there was storytelling. Stories were told not only as entertainment but also as a way of teaching lessons and explaining why things were the way they are. They tell about a culture because they look at the morals and values of traditions and the lessons they teach. Every good story has something you can learn from it, even if it's just the idea that it's good to laugh and be entertained.

Storytelling is an art. Not everyone is able to do it well. Storytellers tell their stories in a way they feel most comfortable. No two storytellers tell the same story the same way. Storytellers use a lot of expression. They not only tell the story by using words but also by using all kinds of body movements. It's fun watching them as they move around while telling their stories. Many storytellers also use props such as hats, animals, other people, or musical instruments to add to their stories.

A famous saying among storytellers is, "I never let the facts get in the way of the truth." This means that although the message is usually true, the facts are sometimes exaggerated.

The best atmosphere for storytelling is a place with no visual or sound distraction, a comfortable audience, and space to move around as you tell the story. If you want to be a successful storyteller, keep practicing, for you may have the talent inside you. Find a story you like and practice telling it in front of a mirror, your pet, your friends, or on a tape. Keep your body moving. You may even be good enough to become a professional storyteller.

In this chapter, we share some of the stories we have heard or read. Each contains a part of Hispanic culture whether it is funny, scary, true, religious, or romantic. We hope you enjoy reading them.

OUR LADY OF GUADALUPE

Do you believe in miracles? If not, then after you read this story you may have to think twice. If you already believe, well,

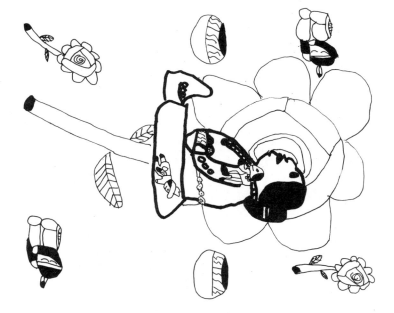

then here's another one to add to your collection.

Most Americans have heard of Our Lady of Guadalupe. She is the patron saint of Mexico. Our Lady of Guadalupe has also appeared in places other than Mexico, and when she does, she takes on the nationality of that country. For example, she was called Our Lady of Fátima when she appeared at Fátima in Portugal. For these reasons, stories about the appearance of "Our Lady" have been carried on for many generations. Her popularity is shown by the large number of churches named after her in the United States. That is why we have included this story. It is a part of the past that will continue to be shared in the future.

In the year 1531, an amazing thing happened in the country now called Mexico. An Indian man named Juan Diego witnessed a miracle that changed his life forever.

On his usual Saturday morning route to the church, Juan Diego heard beautiful music from the hillside of Tepeyac. He followed the sound to the top of the hill where he saw a glistening white cloud with rays of rainbow colors all around. As he came closer, he heard his name being called. Suddenly the cloud split apart, and there before him stood a woman who looked like a beautiful Aztec princess. Right then and there he knew she was a saint, so he fell to his knees in praise.

The woman spoke very softly, saying, "I am the Mother of God, and I have come to give you an important message. Go to the bishop of Mexico and tell him

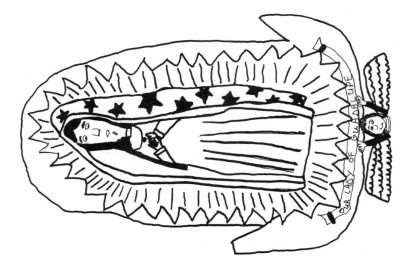

I wish to have a church built in my name, here on this hill, to show my love for all my people."

Juan Diego told her, "I shall do as you wish." He ran as fast as he could to the bishop's house where he had to wait in line for a long time. Finally one of the bishop's helpers questioned Juan Diego as to why he wanted to see the bishop. After explaining what had happened, Juan was able to tell his story to the bishop, who was not sure if he should believe him. He told Juan Diego to come back in a few days so as to give him time to think about everything.

Juan went back to Mary, the Mother of God, and told her he was sorry but that he had failed. The bishop had not believed him. Mary told Juan to go back to the bishop and demand that he build a church on that spot.

Juan returned to the bishop's house in hopes that he would be believed this time. He again had to wait to see the bishop. When Juan saw the bishop, he was not greeted warmly. The bishop told Juan to go back to the Lady and ask her for some kind of proof that the vision was real. Juan rushed back to the hilltop and gave Mary the news. She told Juan to return the next morning for the sign.

When Juan returned home, he found that his uncle was very ill and close to death. All night they tried different ancient remedies to cure his uncle. Nothing seemed to work, so Juan was sent to fetch the priest to give his uncle his last blessings. On the way, he saw the Lady and told her why he couldn't meet with her. She

told him not to worry because his uncle had been cured. She then told him to go to the top of the hill, gather some roses, and bring them back to her. Juan was puzzled because he knew no roses ever grew on the hilltop, especially in winter. But, since he believed in the Lady, he went anyway. At the top of the hill he found a garden of beautiful roses. They still had dew drops on them. He collected as many as he could hold in his cloak and returned to the Lady. The Lady tied his cloak around his neck and gently arranged the roses in it. She told him to take this sign to the bishop but not to show it to anyone else.

Juan took the roses and went swiftly but carefully to the bishop's home. He

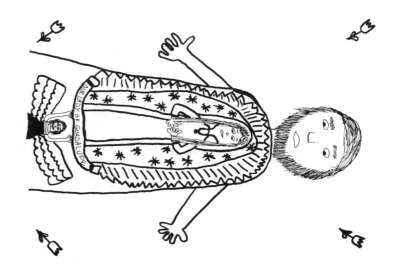

had to wait in line for the third time. The guards tried to get Juan to show them what he was hiding. Juan forgot his promise and showed the guards a small glimpse. Every time they would try to touch a rose, it disappeared into the cloth of the cloak. Not knowing what to do, they rushed him to see the bishop. While in the bishop's private study, Juan opened his cloak and let the roses fall to the floor. Then he noticed that everyone was looking at his cloak. Juan looked down at it and on it saw a beautiful painting of the Lady. The bishop fell to his knees in prayer. The cloak was paraded around town so everyone could witness the great miracle. Soon a small church was built just as the Lady had requested. Many years later, a beautiful cathedral was built in its place and named La Virgin de Guadalupe (The Virgin of Guadalupe). In this cathedral hangs the actual cloak that Juan Diego wore. Even though it is over 400 years old, it shows no signs of falling apart. This made believers out of us.

LA LLORONA [The Weeping Woman]

Have you heard of the boogeyman? In the Hispanic culture, the boogeyman is known as La Llorona. Even though she is feared by many children, adults use her story as a warning to behave your best.

Once, in a small Indian village, there was a girl named Maria. She was the prettiest girl in the village. She swore she would marry the most handsome man. Her *abuelita* (grandmother) said that she should marry a good man and not worry about his looks. Maria didn't pay any attention. She wanted to marry a good-looking man. One day Maria saw a man come to the village. Maria thought that he was very handsome. She asked him his name. He said his name was Gregorio. In about one month, they decided to get married. They had two kids after the marriage. The marriage worked out the first couple of years, but then things started falling apart.

Gregorio started to see other women in front of his wife. He would take his girlfriend to visit his kids at home. He wouldn't even talk to Maria. All he would do was ignore her.

Maria realized that her husband didn't care for her. He only cared for the kids. Soon Maria got jealous of her kids. She got very angry at her husband. She took her kids to the river and drowned them. Maria did this because she thought her husband would love her more without the kids around. When Maria got home, her husband just became angrier. Maria realized what she had done. She went back to the river and began running along the riverbank looking for her children. Paying more attention to the river instead of looking where she was going, she tripped over a root and fell right into the river and smashed her head on a rock. She drowned. Two days later, they found her body by the riverbank. The town priest wouldn't let her be buried in the holy graveyard because she had killed her kids. The priest said to bury her by the river. And to this day, people swear they hear her spirit crying for her children by rivers and lakes. If she sees children, she picks them up and takes them away because she thinks that they are hers. Parents tell their children that if they are not good or don't come home on time, La Llorona will come and get them.

There is a story of Pablo who didn't believe in La Llorona. One day Pablo was playing by the river with his friends. Pablo's friends said it was starting to get late and they should go home. Pablo said, "Why go home? We are having fun." They said La Llorona would get them if they didn't go home. They left, but Pablo stayed because he didn't believe it.

Pretty soon, it got dark and windy. Pablo started to see a white shadow coming through the trees. It started to sound like a ghost. Pablo tried to run, but he couldn't. A voice started saying, "¿Dondé están mis niños?" (Where are my children?) Pablo suddenly saw a white ghost that was flapping through the wind. The ghost, La Llorona, grabbed him up, thinking he was her child. Suddenly, she heard the bell for mass and disappeared in the trees. Pablo ran home as quickly as he

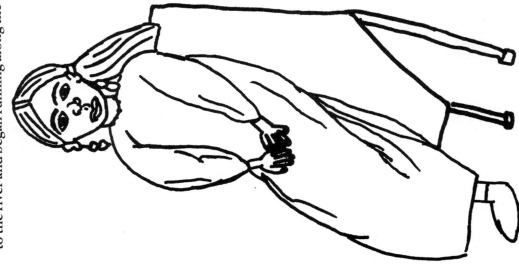

EL GRILLO [The Cricket]

Many stories have a hidden moral or message. In this story, the hidden message deals with stretching the truth. We know it is easy to exaggerate, but a story like this helps remind us how important it is to tell the truth.

In New Mexico, there once lived two men who were neighbors as well as *compadres* (godfathers to each other's children). One of the men was wealthy, hard-working, and well respected. The other was poor because he was lazy and didn't like to work at all. He had the nickname, "The Cricket," because he talked and talked and never was quiet, just like a cricket at night when you're trying to sleep.

The Cricket would brag that he was an *adivino* (fortune-teller) with special powers. Whenever The Cricket would get behind on paying his bills, he would take the rich neighbor's prize-winning mule and hide him in the mountains. His neighbor would come to The Cricket and beg him to use his special powers to find his prize-winning mule. The Cricket would pretend to see a vision. He would tell his compadre where the mule was to be found, and, lo and behold, the mule would be there. The neighbor was so grateful to The Cricket that he would pay all his bills. This happened many times over the years.

One day, the rich neighbor was having lunch with the governor of New Mexico. The governor mentioned to his guest that he had lost his ring. The rich man bragged that his compadre was an adivino

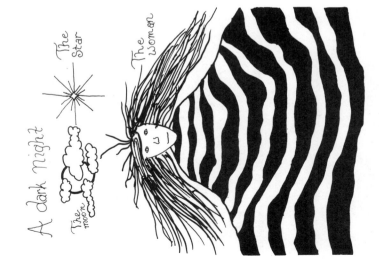

A dark night

The Star

The moon

The Woman

could. When he got home, his mom was mad at him for not coming home on time. He said, fearfully, "Mamá, La Llorona." She didn't believe him and was ready to give him a good shaking when she saw on his shirt five red stains of blood left by La Llorona's fingers. Pablo's mom said that the story of La Llorona was true. So she got all the kids in the village and told them that when it gets dark, you better get home or La Llorona will get you.

This is one of the many versions of La Llorona. We think the original version was told during the time of Cortés.

and could easily find the governor's ring. The governor didn't believe in adivinos but thought it was worth a try. The Cricket was called before the governor. He tried to get out of the situation by denying he had magical powers. He said that he had been lucky once in a while. The governor got real suspicious and decided to put The Cricket on the spot. He locked The Cricket in a room and gave him three days to find his missing ring. If he was able to tell where the ring was, he would be richly rewarded. But, if he wasn't able to find the ring, he would be properly punished.

It just so happened that the ring was not lost but had been stolen by three of the governor's servants. They had it hidden in a safe place until they could sell it and split the money between the three of them.

All day, The Cricket sat next to the window watching the sun rise and set. He tried to think of a way to get out of the situation. At the end of the first day, one of the servants brought The Cricket his supper tray. He set the tray next to The Cricket and started walking toward the door. When The Cricket saw his supper tray, he knew that one of his three days had run out. He said, "Of the three, there goes the first." The servant thought The Cricket was talking about the three servants and not the three days. He ran down to tell the other two servants that The Cricket was truly an adivino. The other two servants tried to convince the first servant there was no such thing as an adivino.

The next evening a different servant brought The Cricket's supper tray. The Cricket again, thinking of the days, said out loud, "Of the three, there goes the second." The second servant ran down the stairs and told the others that it was true. The Cricket did know all about them. He really was an adivino.

On the third evening, the last servant didn't even wait for The Cricket to say anything. He put down the supper tray, fell to his knees, and started confessing. He asked The Cricket not to tell on them. They would do anything he asked. The Cricket was not a stupid man, so when he heard the confession he caught on right away. He told the servant he wouldn't tell if he would take the ring and make sure the governor's fattest goose swallowed it.

When questioned by the governor, The Cricket acted like he had seen a vi-sion. He told the governor that he had seen the ring inside the stomach of his fattest goose. The governor did not believe him but decided to give The Cricket a chance. He was surprised to see the ring when they opened the goose's stomach. He rewarded The Cricket with a bag of gold and the goose for his wife to cook.

A few weeks later, the governor of Chihuahua was talking to the governor of New Mexico. The governor of New Mexico was bragging that in his state there lived a real adivino. The two men began arguing about the truth of adivinos. They finally ended up betting $1,000 over whether The Cricket was a fake or not. The governor of Chihuahua said he would put something in a box and raise it to the top of the flagpole. The Cricket would have to tell what was in the box. If he couldn't, the governor of New Mexico would have to pay the $1,000 to the governor of Chihuahua or vice versa.

The governor of Chihuahua decided to try and trick The Cricket. He took a big box and put a smaller box inside it, then put a smaller box in that one, and so on, until he had a tiny box. He went out into the garden to find something small. Just then, a cricket hopped across the path. He picked up the cricket, put it inside the smallest box, sealed it, and had it pulled up to the top of the flagpole.

The Cricket was brought forth to settle the bet. There was no way for him to escape, because on one side stood the governor of Chihuahua and on the other the governor of New Mexico. To make it even worse, a circle of soldiers surrounded the three.

There stood The Cricket looking up at the box, speechless. An hour passed, then two hours. Finally, the governor of Chihuahua started to chuckle, so the governor of New Mexico got mad and said, "Tell us what's in the box in one minute or I'll have your head!" The Cricket started to stutter, "In the box . . . um, in the box . . . in the box . . ." The governor of Chihuahua was astonished. He thought The Cricket could see there was a box inside a box inside a box. Finally, The Cricket, only thinking of himself, moaned, "Oh, you poor Cricket, they've got you now!" When they opened the box, the governors, of course, found the little cricket in the last box. The governor of Chihuahua handed over the money to the governor of New Mexico and became a true believer. The governor of New Mexico was so pleased that he gave half the money to The Cricket.

While walking home, The Cricket promised never to tell anyone he was an adivino ever again. He soon came upon the neighborhood kids who always teased him. They had filled a gunnysack full of trash and asked him to use his special powers to see what was in the bag. The Cricket was mad, so he yelled, "Leave me alone, that's just a bunch of garbage!" That comment made believers out of the boys. They spread the news, and soon everyone within miles called on The Cricket to find anything they had lost. The Cricket got tired of always being called on, so he moved to someplace where nobody had ever heard of an adivino.

Ratoncitos

LOS RATONCITOS [The Little Mice]

This story about a mouse family is short but has a very important message. We chose it because this message is important for all Americans. See if you can guess what the mother mouse teaches her children.

There once was a mother mouse who had four children. The baby mice were so young that they had never been outside before. One day, they climbed all the way up the hole to see what they were missing. They smelled the air, which was very fresh. They went down the hole and asked their mom if they could take a walk.

She thought it was a wonderful idea, so she led them up the hole and through the grass. Just then, they heard, "Meow, Meow, Hiss!" It was, *el gato*, the cat! She told her children to run. They all ran and hid. The mother knew she had to protect her children so she looked the cat in the eye, stood up real tall, and while shaking her fist said, "Ruff, Ruff, Ruff, Ruff!" The cat got scared by the sound of the barking dog and ran away. The mother mouse told her children to come out. She made sure they were all there by counting them and said, "It always pays to know a second language."

EL PRINCIPE Y LOS PÁJAROS
[The Prince and the Birds]

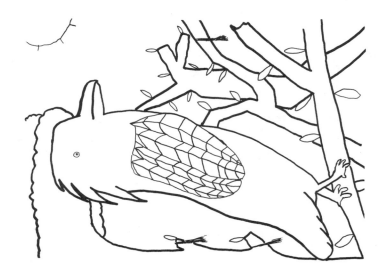

Once there was a Spanish prince whose father locked him in his room. The only two people who came to see him were his father and his tutor.

One day, a dove flew onto his window-sill. The prince fed him some bread and water. Then he put him in a golden cage. The next day, the prince saw the dove crying. The prince asked him what was wrong. The dove told him he wanted to see his loved one. The prince asked the bird what a loved one was. The bird said a loved one was somebody who comforts you. The prince let the bird go.

The next day, the dove came back and told him of a beautiful princess. He was sorry he couldn't take him on his back, but he suggested writing a letter. In a couple of days, the bird came back with an arrow through his heart but a locket around his neck. The prince opened the locket, and there was a picture of the princess. He decided he would set out to find the princess. So the prince escaped from his room by smashing the lock on the door and went to look for the princess.

On his way, the prince ran into some birds who helped him. Phoo was one of them. Phoo said to go to the castle. The prince went to the castle and saw a parrot. The parrot took the prince to see a raven. The raven told him about love.

They went to a castle in a different town, where the princess lived. The parrot went to the princess and told her the prince had come. She told the bird to take her scarf and tell the prince there would be a tournament and she was the prize. The prince was scared because he didn't have any fighting stuff.

Just then, the stork came. He took the prince and the parrot to his cave. He showed him some fighting stuff. The next day, the prince got ready for the tournament. He knew he would not be allowed in the tournament because he was the only one that could beat the king. The king knew this was true, so he ordered his guard to keep the prince out of the tournament. The king really did not want his daughter to marry anyone. The prince killed the guard to get into the tourna-

ment. He beat all the people. Finally, the king himself was to fight the prince. The princess fainted because she was afraid her father might die. When the princess did not awaken, the king hired many people to try and heal her.

One day, the prince dressed up as a wizard and went to the princess. He read to her the poems he had written. She woke up. They stepped onto his magic robe and flew away with the princess. They lived happily ever after.

Note to Readers: If you like these stories, check in your local library, your school or university libraries, or any bookstore for more. Here are just a few suggestions:

The Silver Whistle by Ann Tompert, illustrated by Beth Peck (New York: Macmillan Publishing Co., 1988). This is a beautiful story about a Mexican boy who gives a special gift to the Christ child.

The Day It Snowed Tortillas, retold by Joe Hayes, illustrated by Lucy Jelinek (Santa Fe: Mariposa Publishing, 1990). This book has many folktales from Spanish New Mexico. There's bound to be one you like.

The Lady of Guadalupe written and illustrated by Tomie de Paola (Holiday House, 1980). This is the story of how Our Lady of Guadalupe became the patron saint of Mexico.

Pedro and the Padre, by Verna Aardema, illustrated by Friso Henstra (New York: Dial Books, 1991). This is a story that teaches a lesson about telling lies.

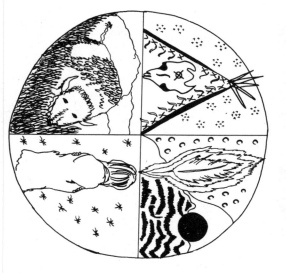

REAL PEOPLE—HISPANICS IN AMERICA TODAY

Real people have their own ways.
They have their own traditions.
They have their own beliefs.
History is in their hearts.

We are proud of this section. The people we interviewed have Cuban, Puerto Rican, Spanish, or Mexican backgrounds. Their lives and heritage tell the story of part of America's history. Some have come from Cuba to find a new life. Others came to the United States as migrant farm workers and improved their lives through education. Some came from families who were here even before the pilgrims. We chose people from all walks of life, professionals and nonprofessionals—people involved in government, business, education, and religious jobs. A group of fifth graders made up questions to ask them because we wanted to know about them, their families, traditions, and values. We asked them

about their favorite childhood memories, their views on prejudice, and their family traditions because we think that this is how we can understand each other better. Again and again, we heard familiar themes that Hispanic families care for each other and have strong religious traditions and a strong desire to serve our country. Our real people shared their own feelings and let us explore their lives. As you read about them, remember that they are just like you and me, not made up or superheroes but normal everyday people who are proud to be Americans.

TINO MENDEZ

When you meet Tino Mendez you will be impressed with his dedication, bravery, friendliness, and sense of humor. He works hard to remind people what freedom is and how important it is to have. He also likes to encourage others to work to keep America free.

Mr. Mendez was born in Cuba in 1944. He was an only child for a long time. When he was twelve, his parents had a daughter. Two years later, they had another son. He loved his little brother and sister very much. Mr. Mendez has many good qualities, especially his pride and his love for freedom. His family means everything to him.

Tino Mendez

and high school. He decided if he was going to get help for his people, he had two choices. He could either stay and try to change things or leave and hopefully return and fight for freedom. It was a painful decision, but he decided he had to leave.

You must realize how hard it would be to get up and leave your family. When he was sixteen, Mr. Mendez filled out many papers, and at seventeen, he took a plane from Cuba to Florida. There he became a refugee. He was in a strange country with a strange language that he hardly knew.

When Mr. Mendez got to the United States, he entered a Catholic Charities camp for children under eighteen years of age. At the camp, a bishop came and took Mr. Mendez to Kansas, where he found a foster home.

In high school, Tino Mendez was a good student. He was involved with the school government and played basketball. His early life was just like that of any one of us, but then a big change took place. In 1959, there was a revolution on the small island of Cuba. Mr. Mendez felt the new government started to control his town

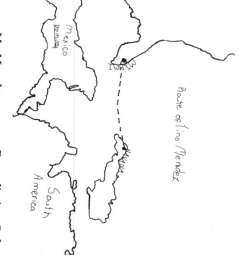

Mr. Mendez went to Benedictine College in Atchison, Kansas, and there he studied math. During this time, he worked at many jobs to try to pay for his education. One of the jobs he had was to work

Bernadette Vigil

on the farm where he was living. He decided to quit that because he was almost killed by a tractor! He then began working at Taco Tico, a fast food place. Then he found out about a job making a lot more money selling encyclopedias door to door. Mr. Mendez graduated from Benedictine College in three years. After that, he didn't have to work any more odd jobs. He went on to get his doctoral degree from the University of Colorado.

Mr. Mendez is now a math teacher at Metropolitan State College in Denver, Colorado. He is married to Mary Ann and has two sons, Matthew and Mark. He is very active in our government because he wants to make certain that our country remains free. He has served in public office and campaigned for many candidates and causes. He does this because he knows the sting of being controlled by the government. His goal is to make people happy by helping them to remain free. His son, Matthew, told us that the best advice from his dad was to be yourself. Mr. Mendez's family is very lucky.

BERNADETTE VIGIL

Bernadette Vigil is a strong individual. She has chosen to remain single and devote her life to preserving the traditions of her heritage through her works of art. Ms. Vigil works hard to bring out her Hispanic heritage in the things she paints. Her art contains a lot of historical and religious ideas. Much of her work is done to help people remember things from the His-

panic culture. Ms. Vigil's feelings about her Hispanic heritage can be seen in what she paints.

Ms. Vigil has lived in Santa Fe, New Mexico, since she was born in 1955. She has five brothers, one sister, and her mother and father, so there are nine people in her family. Her mom and dad taught her to respect other people, because that's the way you're going to want to be treated yourself.

Her parents taught her about religion and how it was important. They also taught her to believe in herself. Her favorite holidays are religious ones, especially Easter and Christmas. She believes in her religion a lot, and her paintings show it. Many of her pictures have crosses, funerals, and resurrections in them.

Ms. Vigil grew up in a wonderful old part of Santa Fe, and her home was made of adobe. On the street where she lived, a lot of other artists lived. When she was little, she played with water snakes and lizards. Her dream was to be a policewoman. That was because she liked the clothes they wore. By sixth or seventh grade, she knew she wanted to be a painter. That might be because several of her relatives were artists. Also, she would watch the artists on her street, with their canvases and paints, painting beautiful pictures.

Ms. Vigil always liked to draw, and her parents were very supportive. She liked art in school. After she graduated from high school, she went to New Mexico Highlands University. Later, she went to the College of Santa Fe and graduated.

Ms. Vigil's house is built on land that her grandparents homesteaded a long time ago. She doesn't plan to marry or have children. She said, ''I always wanted to be an artist, but being an artist is not a traditional role for a Hispanic woman, and in the Hispanic culture, having children is very important. This is my way of having a family. My paintings are a part of me. They are my children. They are my offspring, and I hope that they can inspire others in their lives.''

Bernadette Vigil works all over New Mexico as a painter and really enjoys it. She likes to paint oils and frescoes, paintings on plaster.

We think Ms. Vigil sounds like a very nice and interesting lady. New Mexico is neat, but with Bernadette Vigil there, it's neater.

SIDNEY ATENCIO

Sidney Atencio is the kind of person people would love to be around. He is kind, respectful, and funny. He has dark hair and a mustache. He is tanned and has a low voice, and he is big and very strong. He believes that all people should be respected regardless of their color or beliefs. He feels that his name is something special, and he's proud of it. To Mr. Atencio, learning to spell and say someone's name correctly is a sign of respect. It shows that you care enough to take the time and effort.

Mr. Atencio's relatives were some of the first people to come to the part of

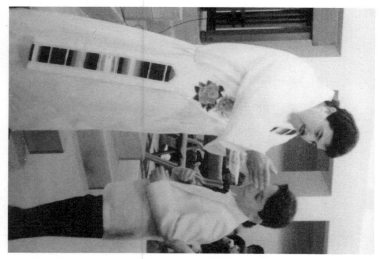

Sidney Atencio

Mexico that is now part of the southern United States. This was even before the pilgrims landed on Plymouth Rock. The family that he grew up in was very small, with three children, but when his whole family got together, it was completely different. In fact, people would walk by and say, "Is that all one family?"

Mr. Atencio must believe in education because he has gone to school for twenty-seven years. During the last four years of his schooling, he studied to be a deacon in the Catholic church. Mr. Atencio adores books, and he works in the Denver Public Library.

Mr. Atencio loves family gatherings. We think he likes family gatherings so much because he is a deacon who helps people. He has been a deacon for four years. He works mainly with the homeless at the Samaritan Center. He counsels many people, such as husbands and wives with marriage problems and much more.

Mr. Atencio has a family of his own. He has a wife and two sons named after famous Hispanics. His sons are called Francisco and Diego. His wife, Lillian, is a big part of his life. She works in the post office. (But it's not her fault the mail is late!)

An old tradition in the Hispanic Catholic church is called quinceanera (fifteenth birthday). This is when a girl celebrates that she is becoming a woman. As girls approach the age of fifteen, they take preparation classes. In these classes, they talk about friendship, dating, drugs, suicides, and family communication. You don't have to be Hispanic to do this. Mr. Atencio is carrying on this tradition by holding classes and preparing the girls and their families for this ceremony. It is very important to him that the girls learn about themselves and their culture. He feels this is a great way to keep tradition alive as well as help the young girls lead healthier, happier lives. At the end of the classes, the girls' families and friends celebrate the quinceanera. The girls wear a white dress like a bride, and each one has fourteen escorts (like bridesmaids and groomsmen) who march in procession. During the mass, the girl has to make a speech, "Who Am I?" Her parents talk about her to the guests. Mr. Atencio said a lot of people cry because it is so beautiful. After the ceremony, the girls have officially turned "sweet fifteen."

Mr. Atencio spends a lot of his time teaching people to be proud of who they are. It is important to him that people know about themselves and their heritage and celebrate their beginnings. He wants people to pass on the traditions that they have through their families and their heritage.

BENNIE AND LIL RAZO

Bennie and Lil Razo live in Chillicothe, Illinois. Both of their families came from Mexico. We chose to talk to these people because their family life illustrates a very important part of the Hispanic heritage. They have a loving, caring, very close family. They have worked hard to keep close and show their family that happiness in

Bennie and Lil Razo

life and family is the most important thing to work for.

Mr. Razo's father, Thomas, came to the United States when his uncle got him a job working for the Sante Fe Railroad. Mr. Razo's uncle was a foreman on the railroad. Thomas moved to Chillicothe where the railroad job was. Later, when his father married, he and his wife moved into a boxcar to live. The railroad company offered only boxcars for houses to people who hadn't worked for the company very long. If you had worked on the railroad for a long time, you could live in a brick house.

Bennie Razo was born in this boxcar and lived there until he was eighteen years old. Then he joined the military and was sent to Korea. Mr. Razo later went to college, but before he could finish, he left because he needed to take care of his new family.

Mr. Razo married Lil. They had two girls and two boys. He now works as a cus-

todian. Mrs. Razo is a housewife and also works on an assembly line. They taught their kids what their parents taught them. This was to show respect for everyone, especially their parents, and not to be ashamed of who you are.

When Mr. Razo was a kid, he liked going to the movies with his parents once a month. When Mrs. Razo was a kid, she liked going to the country, taking long walks, picking blackberries, and playing games. She remembers that once when she was young, a boy teased her and her girl-friend about being Hispanic. Her brother came out of the house one day and scared him away. He never teased them again. Mrs. Razo doesn't think people are as pre-judiced as they used to be.

Mr. Razo's hero was his high school coach, George Taylor. Coach Taylor was there for Mr. Razo when he had trouble in school. He made him stay in school even though it was difficult for him. The special people who helped Mr. Razo become who he is today are his dad and Coach Taylor. When Mr. Razo was in high school, he wanted to be a coach and a teacher.

Mrs. Razo's parents were married in Mexico. They worked their way north and eventually emigrated to the United States. This means they left their home in Mexico to live in the United States. Many people left their homelands because of wars or sickness. Sometimes they left for political or religious reasons. Mrs. Razo's family came to find better jobs. Her family paid a penny each to cross the border. This was a processing fee for paperwork.

As a young girl, Mrs. Razo wanted to

Left to right: Rosie Valdez, Pete Valdez, Sr., Mr. and Mrs. John Gore

be a cosmetologist when she grew up. Mrs. Razo's brother, Joe, was her hero because he taught her to stand up for herself and be proud of who she is. The special person who helped her become who she is today is her mother.

Today, Mr. and Mrs. Razo's four children are grown up and starting their own families. They have all worked hard to be what they are. Each one has spent time in school trying very hard to succeed in life. Jacqueline works in a bank. Renee works at the Area Agency on Aging, a state-funded program. Tom teaches in southern Illinois. David works in a restaurant and goes to college.

Mrs. Razo's advice to Hispanic youth is to be proud of yourself and "go out in life and do the best you can." Mr. Razo's words of wisdom are, "Study, because no one can ever take your education away from you." Their goals are to live a happy life with a happy family, and they're doing just that! The Razos know they have been successful because now, as their children start their own lives, they, too, are working hard to carry on the family traditions.

PETE VALDEZ

We chose to write about Pete Valdez because he represents a good example for Hispanics in America. Mr. Valdez served our country by fighting in World War II as a member of the United States Army. It has been estimated that nearly 500,000 Hispanic people fought in World War II as part of the armed forces. Mr. Valdez feels very strongly for our country and fought very hard to keep it the way it is.

Mr. Valdez was one of six to win the Silver Helmet Award on April 21, 1991. He is the first Mexican-American to win this award, which is a trophy that has a small, shiny helmet about the size of a small clock on a thick dish. It is a replica of the G.I. steel helmet soldiers used in World War II. In fact, it looks just like the helmet Mr. Valdez used to heat his water in when he fought in World War II.

The Silver Helmet Award for performing excellent service for our country is given by the AMVETS organization. This is an organization of American veterans of World War II, Korea, and Vietnam. The awards are given to people who have worked hard and made a difference in areas such as defense, patriotism, rehabilitation, congressional service, and peace. All people can be nominated for this award. The Silver Helmet Award is sometimes called the Oscar Award for veterans.

That means that it is like the awards for movie stars except it is for veterans.

Pete Valdez was born in Los Angeles, California. He is the oldest of twenty-one brothers and sisters. There are three sets of twins in his family. His family was poor. So they could earn money for the family, Mr. Valdez and his brother would shine shoes for the people who got off the boats at the docks. He and his brother would hide their shoeshine kits behind the bushes while they were at school because they didn't want to take them into the school. When they got out of school, they would go to the boats. Mr. Valdez and his brother would also make money by picking up bananas and wood that dropped from the crates that came from the boats. They put both things in their little red wagon and sold them for nickles and dimes. They would also sell newspapers at the dock.

Mr. Valdez's dad worked full-time as a stevedore (someone who works on docks loading ships) and part-time as a mechanic. He used to help his father in the garage. His hands would get all greasy. He scrubbed and scrubbed, but he couldn't get his hands clean. Other kids used to tease him about being dirty. Mr. Valdez would fight or run away.

When he was a little boy, Mr. Valdez wanted to be a tank driver. He was so interested in this job that he enlisted in the army when he was seventeen. He went to tank-driving school in Ft. Hood, Texas. He was very happy to go to tank school, but then he had some bad luck. One day when he was in school, they called fifteen peo-ple out. He was one of them. Mr. Valdez got the news that he was going to the South Pacific to man a machine gun. He never got to drive a tank, but he was proud to serve his country. He was lucky and got out of the war without a scratch.

After World War II, Mr. Valdez knew he needed an education. So, when he got home, he applied for the G.I. Bill to go to school. The government created this bill to set aside money for military people to be retrained after they left the service. Mr. Valdez learned to work in a machine shop and design tools and got a job in a machine shop. He also was the security guard. When he had extra time at night, Mr. Valdez would learn how to use each machine. After one year, Mr. Valdez went to work at Hughes Aircraft. He worked his way up until he was a project manager. Then he started hiring people from Hispanic neighborhoods to work at Hughes.

Mr. Valdez married his high school sweetheart, who was his next door neighbor. Her name is Rosie. Marrying Rosie was a tremendous help. Mr. Valdez says that she is the "light of his life." Mr. and Mrs. Valdez had four sons. They all wanted to be in the service. Three got to serve. The other one really wanted to serve, too, but didn't get to because he had medical problems. Now he's a minister. Two of the sons served in the army, and the other served in the air force.

Mr. Valdez is a proud American who has contributed in many ways to his country and his family. He fought in World War II and then came back to help other soldiers who fought in wars. He volunteers many, many hours to make our country a good place. Because we think Mr. Valdez is special, his advice is important to us. He believes the family is important and wants everyone to respect their parents and elders. He told us to be honest with everyone and to try very hard to get an education so you can make more of yourself.

ALICIA FERNANDEZ-MOTT

We talked with Alicia Fernandez-Mott, a very important advocate for migrant farm workers. She is a supervisor for the Division of Migrant and Seasonal Farmworker Programs, U.S. Department of Labor, Washington, D.C. She works with the Job Training Partnership Act. This act is meant to provide education for adult farm workers so they can get year-round and full-time work.

Alicia Fernandez-Mott was a migrant worker herself for several years. In doing her job as an advocate for migrant farm workers, she has met both Cesar Chavez and Baldamar Velasquez, who is the president of the Farm Labor Organizing Committee. Both of these people work hard to get migrant farm workers a lot of the services they need and deserve, like health care and clean facilities in which to live. Ms. Fernandez-Mott feels she works with Mr. Chavez and Mr. Baldamar in helping the farm workers. She says that their strength and determination for the needs of farm workers is something that she shares with them since she, too, has lived as a migrant farm worker.

Alicia Fernandez-Mott

Alicia traveled with her family along the migrant streams from the age of four, off and on, until she was twenty. She actually started working at the age of six by picking tomatoes and cucumbers. This was hard work because she wasn't very strong.

Because she dropped out of school at the age of sixteen, Ms. Fernandez-Mott has had to work very hard to get where she is now. She went back to school when she was thirty. She received her G.E.D. and then went to college. She got her degree in business.

Ms. Fernandez-Mott had lots of information about migrant farm workers. This is just some of what she shared with us.

Migrant farm workers are people who have very determined work ethics resulting from having to earn their keep.

They are people who have very little education or work skills. They don't speak English and so they have a difficult time finding a job. They work as migrant farm workers because they don't need to speak English and they don't need to have any schooling. Since this kind of job keeps a person moving, it is next to impossible to get any education or skills to learn a different job. So these people end up being migrant workers forever. The kids end up in the same situation as their parents. They do not have an education or skills, and they also have very little knowledge of the English language.

Working as a migrant farm worker is a very difficult situation. These workers travel in migrant streams, routes to different harvest places that workers follow. They travel in crowded trucks. Sometimes the workers travel with their family, but at other times they are separated. The trucks are filled with people of all ages. Sometimes they travel for two and a half to three days straight. The workers don't know much about where they go. They judge the distance by state borders, not by miles. When they stop at their farms to work, the workers are packed tight into small cabins that don't always have indoor plumbing. They are supposed to have a refrigerator, but often they don't work. Small propane stoves are also supplied, but the migrant workers have to supply the propane fuel and sometimes they can't afford it.

There are a lot of health problems that come with the job. There are pesticides, which are bug killers that can harm people. Pesticides hurt your lungs, eyes, and skin. The type of labor involved requires a lot of stooping, bending, and lifting. All of these movements can hurt the joints in your body. There are a few clinics for the workers, but these are not free, and a lot of the time the workers can't afford it. Also, these clinics don't cover all of the problems that the workers might have. They are limited in what they can cure. A lot of the health problems of farm workers go uncared for.

Migrant workers are paid by how much they pick. Their employers pay them a certain amount of money for each basket or bushel of food they gather. The amount of money they make is different at each stop. If the crops are good, then they will earn more money. Since their earnings are so uncertain, farm workers can't save money. They also don't get extra money to cover the cost of gas to get from one place to another.

Ms. Fernandez-Mott has been helping migrant workers so they won't have the same problems as she did with getting an education so that she could get a better paying job. She works hard to set up programs for training and other kinds of education. If the parents get educated, then their children don't have to travel all the time. They can afford more things and can also get their own education. She is very determined to get Hispanic people to set goals and measure their achievements. Ms. Fernandez-Mott feels Hispanic people need more education to earn respect in the American society. She also wants to show other people about

Hispanic heritage and its value to the United States.

SYLVIA TELLES

Sylvia Telles is a person who has spent her whole life helping people. This takes faith, courage, and love, which she has found in the roots of her family's past.

Three flags have flown over New Mexico. They are the Spanish flag, the Mexican flag, and now the American flag. Miss Telles's ancestors have been there the whole time. They were the settlers, ranchers, deputies, ditch riders, and ordinary people of their time. Her family never moved to America. The land they owned became the United States territory in 1848. Even though the American flag flew over the land, her family were not considered citizens. They were still called subjects under the king of Spain.

Miss Telles's great-grandfather, on her dad's side, was a cattle rancher east of Las Cruces, New Mexico. Her mother's grandfather owned a ranch next to a lake named after them—Lucero Lake. The original farmhouse is still on this property and can be seen today. It is near the White Sands National Monument. Miss Telles's ancestors did many great things. Her great-uncle was the sheriff of Las Cruces in 1908 when Pat Garrett shot Billy the Kid. You can read all about Pat Garrett surrendering to Sheriff Lucero in some history books today. That's neat.

Miss Telles has a mom and dad, a brother, and three sisters. They all grew up in Las Cruces. They were brought up with a deep respect for their family, their religion, and their elders. She remembers a time when her dad was having a special guest over. Miss Telles's dad made her practice how to greet his friend. She pretended like her dad was the guest and practiced and practiced until she could do it right. When the man came, she gave him a very respectful greeting.

Miss Telles also was taught to be respectful to older people in her family. When her Uncle Margarito was around, he would ask her to get him a glass of water, and she would go directly to the kitchen. She would walk back to her uncle and stand next to him with her arms folded.

Sylvia Telles

When her uncle was finished, he gave the glass back to her, and then she would return it to the kitchen.

They had some special neighbors named Marquez who owned a tortilla factory. Some afternoons, Grandma Marquez would have them kneel and pray the rosary with her. If they were all behaving while she took care of them, occasionally they were allowed to go to the tortilla factory. There they would get a hot tortilla with butter on it!

Another thing Miss Telles's parents shared with her was their faith, but she was not always as close to God as she is now. When she was in college, she went on a church "Teen Day," and she heard some people from her school talking about God. She then realized how important she thought God really was. Miss Telles lives in St. Paul, Minnesota, today. She works for the National Evangelization Teams (NET). In 1987, she volunteered for ten months to travel with other people and talk to youth about God. Then she was hired in 1988 to help train the NET people. Miss Telles has even traveled to Australia for her work. She is very grateful and excited because NET is beginning to work with more Hispanics. They have a team that went to Honduras this year, and they work in areas of the United States where there are many Hispanic people. Miss Telles really has a heart for what she calls her *raza* (her race).

If you find Miss Telles today, she may be visiting with her family. They are very proud of her. She may be wearing a southwestern T-shirt that she made. Miss Telles and her family might even be looking through old Wild West magazines about her uncles, the deputies and sheriffs of the old times. She says it's fun.

THE MARTINEZ FAMILY

Martinez is a very common name in Hispanic culture. Today, there are four generations alive in this one Martinez family of 75 members which began with Maria and Juan Martinez. All of them live less than 150 miles from each other in the state of Colorado. By interviewing 7 members of this extended family, we were able to see the changes each generation made through time with things like traditions, education, careers, and holidays.

The first generation is Maria Martinez, the great grandmother. Next we talked to her daughter, Odelia Martinez Quintana, and her son, Jose Martinez. They are the second generation. For the third generation, we interviewed Diana Quintana Martinez and Jose Martinez, Jr. The fourth generation is made up of Jose III and Julio, who are Maria Martinez's great-grandchildren.

The First Generation

Maria Martinez was born on April 6, 1909, in a small town in New Mexico. She remembers always wanting to play, but she always had a lot of work to do. Maria went to a very small school until the third grade, when she left school to help at home with the family.

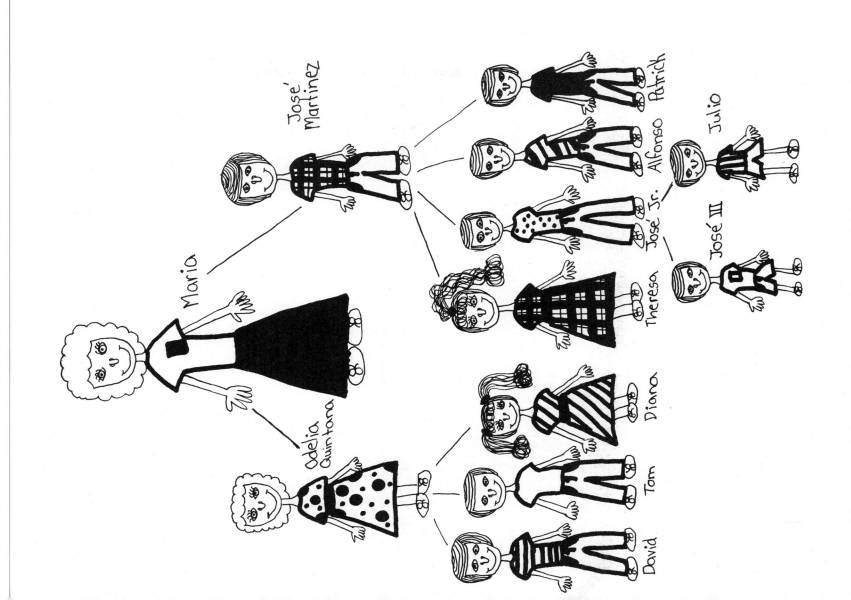

When Maria was 16, she married Juan P. Martinez, who was 27 years old. Mr. and Mrs. Martinez had some land in New Mexico where they raised their children before coming to Colorado. In a very small home, they had fourteen children. Two of the fourteen children died. The older children would help their mother take care of the younger children.

Mr. and Mrs. Martinez moved from New Mexico to Colorado with their family. Shortly after this time, Mr. Martinez died. Some of the kids wanted to finish high school, but they were not able to because they had to work and help support the family.

Maria's home is close to some of her children. The home is decorated with many pictures of her family. There are also many statues and pictures of saints. Mrs. Martinez does a lot of things the same way she did when she lived in her small home in New Mexico. She washes her clothes by hand and hangs them on her clothesline. She makes her own special type of beef jerky and hangs it in a bedroom to dry. She still makes all of her own tortillas and breads from scratch and still cans fruits and vegetables. Maria says she has lived a very full life and that she is very happy.

The Second Generation

Odelia Martinez was born in 1928. She is Mrs. Martinez's oldest living daughter. Odelia went to school until she was fourteen. After leaving school, she moved to Denver with her cousins and got a job. When she was 21 years old, she married Ben Quintana. They had three kids named David, Thomas, and Diana.

Mr. Quintana worked as a mechanic, and Mrs. Quintana stayed home to care for her kids. Once the Quintanas wanted a new car seat for their car, so they made it all by themselves. Other people liked the work they did and asked if they could make cushions and seat covers for them.

The word spread about their good work, and soon Mr. Quintana quit his job to begin the new business with Mrs. Quintana. This business, called Ben's Upholstery, is still run by their family today in Denver, Colorado! Mrs. Quintana only finished the eighth grade, but she must be a pretty smart lady to have a family and a good career at the same time.

Mrs. Quintana and her husband still live in the same house they bought when they were first married. Just like her mother, she still cans her own fruits and vegetables and makes her own tortillas. When we asked her if there was something about her past that she would change if she could, she said that she would like to have known how to borrow more money when she was starting her business. She is a very happy person and is very proud of her family.

Jose Martinez was born in 1936. He is one of Mrs. Martinez's seven sons and a brother to Maria. One of his favorite memories is when he and his brothers and sisters played with homemade guitars.

Mr. Martinez went to school until he was in the eighth grade. He then went to work on a farm. When he was 19 years old, he got married to Altagracia Baca,

Standing, left to right: Odelia Martinez Quintana, Diana Quintana, José D. Martinez I, José A. Martinez II; Sitting: Julio R. Martinez, María Martinez, José A. Martinez III

who was 18. Jose and Altagracia had four kids. Mr. Martinez went back to school to get his G.E.D. (that means high school equivalency diploma). Later, Mr. Martinez became the manager of a farm. His job helped his wife to go back to school, too, and earn her G.E.D. After she got her diploma, she went to college to become a teacher. Mr. Martinez is now a field worker for a chemical company. He belongs to the Knights of Columbus and is always ready to help the community. Mrs. Martinez is a teacher in an elementary school. Mr. Martinez had advice for us. He said to stay in school. He wished that he had stayed in school when he was younger.

The Third Generation

Diana Quintana was born in 1960. She is the youngest of three children. When she was growing up, she helped her mother with the chores at home and at her parents' business. She also played in a nearby creek catching bugs and play acting the Miss America Pageant with friends. She says her childhood was lots of fun. She remembers celebrating Christmas with a decorated tree and waiting for Santa Claus to come and leave gifts. When she graduated from high school, she got married to Michael Martinez and went to college for one year. She is now an office manager for an insurance company. Diana doesn't have any children, but she and her husband have traveled a lot since they got married.

Jose Martinez, Jr., was born in 1958. When he was a little boy, he helped his father on the farm feeding the cattle and riding on the tractors. He was in Boy Scouts and played baseball. He says that he had a very happy childhood.

Jose, Jr., grew up believing that Santa Claus came on December 25 to leave gifts for good boys and girls. He did not know about the Three Kings and January 6th. He wants to help his own kids understand how religion and Christmas go together, and he is trying to help them celebrate the Day of the Three Kings.

Jose, Jr., finished high school and college. Then he married Annette Acevedo and had two children, Jose III and Julio. He was the first person in his family to graduate from college. Jose, Jr., says that he has more opportunities in his life than his father did. He is now a counselor in a high school and has a master's degree.

The things that are the most important to Jose, Jr., are health, family, education, and remembering where you came from so that you can be as good a person as possible.

The Fourth Generation

Jose III (born in 1985) and Julio (born in 1988) are the sons of Jose Martinez, Jr. They are learning from their parents the importance of their heritage. As young as the boys are, they are already saving for college. Jose III and Julio say, "If you want to be cool, stay in school."

Changes over the Four Generations

Families have gotten smaller in number. They have acquired degrees in higher education, and careers have changed. There are more choices for both men and women. Holidays are still celebrated and still have some of the same traditions they did eighty years ago!

BISHOP ROBERTO GONZALES

Many Hispanics are gaining leadership roles across our country. Bishop Roberto Gonzales, a leader in the Roman Catholic church, became a bishop at the young age of 38.

Bishop Gonzales was born in Elizabeth, New Jersey, on June 2, 1950. Although he was born in New Jersey, he grew up in San Juan, Puerto Rico. He came from a very large family. There are nine kids in his family. He is the oldest. With his parents, that is a total of eleven people. He has many aunts, cousins, and uncles, too.

Like most of us, Bishop Gonzales has a hero, but it's not Rambo, Superman, or Batman. The bishop's hero was his father, because he always knew what was going on in the family and he was around when the family needed him. The bishop said that his father had a ton of love for the family.

His mother's grandmother, Carmen Nieves, was also a very special person to him. She taught Bishop Gonzales and his brothers and sisters to take care of the graves of their relatives. They kept the graves pretty by pulling weeds and planting more flowers. This is very important to the people in Puerto Rico. It is part of a tradition that helps people remember that family love goes beyond life. Just because someone isn't here doesn't mean you can't still show them love and respect. They do this by cleaning the graves and respecting their burial sites.

Some of the favorite holidays that the Gonzales family celebrated were Christmas, New Year's, festival days, and also Holy Thursday. On Holy Thursday, Bishop Gonzales's father would read the passage

Weston, Massachusetts, which is a town west of Boston.

Bishop Gonzales is not married like our moms and dads are, but in another way, he's married to the people that he helps in the church. He wears a special ring that shows that he is a bishop and that he is true to the church.

Bishop Gonzales feels that all languages are God's languages and you should be proud of your culture. He says, "Love your roots, love yourselves, love your family, and love all people." We think he is a great Hispanic leader.

Bishop Roberto Gonzalez

of the Last Supper from the Bible. After reading the Bible, the family would eat lamb and matzo (matzo is bread made without yeast), and each child would get a small sip of wine. The bishop also likes the tradition called the nine days of Christmas. During this time a person can go to church at 5:00 in the morning, sing Christmas folksongs in church, and then after church, the whole family would drink hot chocolate. This celebration is called Misa de Aginaldo. Puerto Ricans say that it is like a gift to go to church.

When he was little, the bishop wanted to be a doctor, a lawyer, and a police officer, just like other kids, but by the time he was fourteen, he knew he wanted to be a priest. In 1964, he went to New York to a Franciscan seminary. He finished high school, went to college, then theology school. After he was a priest, he studied sociology at Fordham University in New York City. Now, at age 41, Roberto Gonzales is a Roman Catholic bishop in

HOMERO E. ACEVEDO II

Homero E. Acevedo II is an executive with the American Telephone and Telegraph Company (AT&T). Mr. Acevedo has used his good education and his ability to communicate well in English and Spanish to become one of the youngest managers of the AT&T National Bilingual Center in San Antonio, Texas. There are lots of things we can learn from Mr. Acevedo.

Mr. Acevedo is very close to his family. Born in 1961, he is the youngest child. His family includes his late father, Homero, Sr., his mother, Maria, his two sisters, Annette and Angelique, and his twin brothers, Hugo and Hector.

When Mr. Acevedo was young, he was never lonesome with his brothers and sisters around. He especially remembers going down the stairs Christmas morning when his father made home movies and blinded him with bright floodlights.

Homero E. Acevedo II

His father and mother always encouraged him to get a good education, share with others, love others, work hard, and be all that he could be. They were also a good example for him. His parents were and still are his heroes. Some day, he hopes to have a beautiful family of his own.

Mr. Acevedo's parents gave him advice about how to handle teasing and prejudice. His father told him that if someone thought there was something wrong with him because he was Hispanic, then that person must not have been educated very well and should be ignored. So, that is exactly what he has done. He is proud of who he is.

Mr. Acevedo's dad taught him what goals are and helped him achieve some. One of his goals was to become an outstanding athlete. He did, and his favorite sports were soccer, baseball, and basketball. At one point, he played semiprofessional soccer. He loves Chicago teams, especially the Bears, Bulls, Cubs, and Blackhawks. Although sports are an important part of Mr. Acevedo's life, they never became his main goal.

The most important goal was to get a good education. Mr. Acevedo realized that a good education would open many doors for him in the future. In high school, he studied hard and made excellent grades. He then graduated from the University of Denver. While in college, he had a chance to study in Spain. By being one of the top academic students, he got to meet the king of Spain, Juan Carlos.

Mr. Acevedo knew that he needed to be ready to move to different parts of the country to advance in his career. He moved to New Jersey for training. He was in charge of testing a new billing system and a new computer system that would take care of eighty million residential customer accounts. This was a great responsibility.

After six months of testing the computer system, he was moved to San Antonio, Texas. There he is an operations manager in charge of the International Communications Service Center. Many office managers report to him. There are about 175 people in his department. He makes sure that everything runs smoothly.

Mr. Acevedo is able to communicate with people very well. He can speak and write fluent English and Spanish. He feels very lucky to know two languages and believes it has helped him be a successful executive. He says, "Anyone can be a success if they are secure with themselves, ready to move, and an achiever."

Mr. Acevedo's advice to young people is to be proud of who you are and try to show it. Love your family, and listen to their advice. Always work hard, stay in school, and make a good life for yourself.

MARY ANN A. ZAPATA

Mary Ann Zapata has dedicated her life to education. She not only worked hard to overcome obstacles and achieve a good education for herself but now she works to get this for others.

As a teacher, she is a very catchy woman! She catches children's attention by telling them about how she was raised and how to get a good education. She teaches her students to get along with one another, to stay in school, and not to judge people by their color or race.

Could you imagine moving almost every year? As a child, Mary Ann Zapata grew up in a migrant family. She lived in Texas until she was four. If you're wondering what a migrant family is, it is a family that moves a lot. The family moves a lot because crops ripen at different times of the year so the family must go to different farms even if they are in other states.

Mrs. Zapata was born on November 25, 1943, in Texas. When she was four, she moved to Walla Walla, Washington. Each year, her migrant family moved to Oregon and then to California. Then, she and her family moved back to Walla Walla because that was like their home base.

When Mrs. Zapata was in first grade, the teacher showed prejudice and did not

Mary Ann Zapata helping Hispanic students with reading in English

like her. Mrs. Zapata only knew how to speak Spanish. The teacher ignored her and did not want to teach her how to speak English. Even the kids were mean. They teased her and also made faces and called her names. She had only one friend in first grade. However, the other kids told Mrs. Zapata's friend that she was Hispanic and to stop being her friend, so soon she had no friends. Then she did not want to go to school, but her parents made her go anyway. In second grade, the teacher was warmer and kinder and taught her to speak English. When Mrs. Zapata was older, she wanted to be a teacher because she didn't want kids to be treated poorly.

Is your father your hero? Mrs. Zapata's father was and still is her hero. When she learned English, she wanted to teach her parents. Since her father had to work, she would read to him every night. If you are wondering why her dad is her hero, it is because his opinions helped her to get a good education and to stay in school. He would take her out into the field and show her how tough life would be if she did not get a good education by staying in school.

Mrs. Zapata's favorite holidays have always been Christmas and Easter. She likes spending time with her family and relatives and has realized the importance of family.

Mrs. Zapata has five daughters. The oldest is married, the two youngest still live at home, and the other two are off at college. Her daughters' ages are 10, 13, 19, 23, and 25. Mrs. Zapata teaches her kids to get along, not to judge people by their looks, and to remember to treat other people the way you would like to be treated.

Mrs. Zapata went to college to learn how to be a teacher because her younger years were uncomfortable. She went to college for five years and is still going so she can learn more about how to be a better teacher. She feels sadness in her heart when she hears somebody is going to drop out of school. Mrs. Zapata is kind, lovable, sensible, reasonable, and trusting! As she would say, "Stay in school and get a good education!"

CARLOS FLORES, M.D.

Are you proud of being Hispanic? Well, Dr. Carlos Flores is! Don't you think it would be exhausting to be an emergency medi-

cine doctor, taking care of people who come to the hospital emergency room for help? This is exactly what Carlos Flores, M.D., does.

Dr. Flores explained that it took a lot of hard work and ambition to get where he is today. When he was in ninth grade, he got very interested in biology, and that is when he set his goal to become a doctor. He went to Northwestern University in Chicago for four years and studied very hard as a pre-med student. Then he went to medical school at New York University for four more years. After that, he did two years of residency and additional training in emergency medicine. He has been an emergency medicine doctor for seven years in the New York City area. He says he still has to continue to read and learn about all of the new advances and discoveries in his field.

Dr. Flores's job involves many differ-

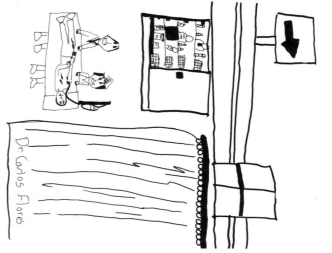

Dr. Carlos Flores

ent kinds of medicine. He does everything from helping with sore throats and ear infections to diagnosing broken bones and taking care of people who have been in accidents or have had heart attacks. His most memorable experience was when a girl was having a very bad asthma attack. She wasn't breathing very well and was turning blue. Dr. Flores helped bring her pink color back, and she was able to breathe well again.

Dr. Flores was born February 23, 1956. He forgets how quickly time flies. During our interview, his wife laughed at him because often it seemed to him as if something happened two years ago, when it was really ten. He grew up in a suburb of San Juan, Puerto Rico, and went to George O. Robinson School from kindergarten through twelfth grade. When he was younger, he liked to play basketball. His idol and hero as a kid was Jerry West, who was one of the L.A. Lakers' basketball players. He had a friend named Billy, and to Dr. Flores it seemed like they would stay at each other's houses every other weekend. He was also an Eagle Scout, which is the highest level in Boy Scouting, and he went to two jamborees, which are big Boy Scout meetings. One was in Idaho, and the other was in Japan.

Although he is the only child of his parents, Cristina and Carlos, he grew up with a very large extended family. This includes about forty cousins, aunts, and uncles. As a boy, he liked to travel with his parents to the United States. His parents speak Spanish and English. He would like to teach his children Spanish.

Dr. Flores lived in Puerto Rico from 1956 to 1982. His ancestors lived in Puerto Rico also. In Puerto Rico, Dr. Flores and his family did not have any problems with prejudiced people because almost everybody there is Hispanic. However, he says being Puerto Rican affected his life when he went away to college. There he had to overcome the prejudice some people had against Hispanics. Dr. Flores proved them wrong by just being himself, and they soon found out that he was just like one of them.

Dr. Flores now lives in the New York City area. He is married and has two small boys. His wife is Jewish, so his family celebrates all the Jewish holidays as well as Christmas, New Year's, and the Day of the Three Kings. His favorite foods are rice and beans and pasta. Although he does not have any hobbies, he does a lot of work around the house, such as redoing the bathroom and rebuilding the backyard deck. He also likes to spend time with his children and his wife. Dr. Flores says that his goals are to be a good father and husband and to be the best doctor he can be.

Dr. Flores's advice to others is to stay in school, set goals, and don't let anyone stop you.

STUDENT AUTHORS

Adrianne Aleman
Dominic Atencio
James B. Barela
Nichole Christine Bargas
Bryan Brammer
Kevin Brand
Kimberly Burnell
Rachel Caliga
Rocio M. Chavez
Nicole Cook
Anastasia Cordova
Christopher deBree
Olivia deBree
Karina deOliviera
Brandon Dudley
Jennifer Flores-Sternad
Asia Garcia
Jaya Garcia
Amanda Gomez
Lanette Gonzales
Sergio Gonzales
Vanessa Gonzales
Brittany Hanson
Jenna Maria Helms
Heather Herburger
Jared Daniel Herrera
Cambri Hilger
Maria Hodge
Troy D. Holder
Aimee Hull
Christopher Husted
Amy Jessop
Ryan Joyce
Justin Juarez
Greg Karsten
Whitney Kastelic
Perry D. Kline
Michael Laydon
Ben Lowry
Aynber E. Mackenzie
Fernando Manrique

Gonzalo Manrique
Alisha Martinez
Erica J. Martinez
Melissa Medrano
Amber A. Montoya
Jacob Montoya
Daniel Murphy
Harrison Nealey
April Padilla
Christina Marie Padilla
Roberto Padilla
Clint A. Parker
Vickie Pepper
Josh Jesus Pettit
Emily Phelan
Brian Quinn
Victor Quinonez, Jr.
Cliff M. Rodriguez
Danelle Marie Rodriguez
Desiree Marie Rodriguez
Sarah Lynn Romero
Lance Ruybal
Nick Sanchez
Matthew Sandoval
Valerie Karla Schultz
Jennifer Shouse
Ricky Stevens
Magaret Stillman
Kimberly Sturk
Addie Jo Suazo
Donna Swigert
Laura Swigert
Anne Tatarsky
Kimberly Trujillo
Judy Beth Urteaga
Candace Elisa Valencia
Tommy C. Venard
Lara K. Vette
Angie Wegher
Brandon Weinberger
Jenny L. Wrzesinski

TEACHER PARTICIPANTS

Angelique Acevedo (Hispanic Consultant)
Annette M. Acevedo-Martinez
Alex Gill Balles
Pia R. Borrego
Jean Tiran Cable
Helen T. Cozzens (Co-Director)
Judith H. Cozzens (Co-Director)
Mary Ann Garcia-Pettit
Lorraine Gutierrez
Marsha Herald
Jan Lahlum
Jerry Lassos
Martin Laydon
Tria Lopez
Jean Makalusky-Martinez
Jose A. Martinez
Maria Ortiz-Venard
Melanie Shioya-Davis
Sherry Stumbaugh
Harvey Torrey
Andra Vette

OTHER PARTICIPANTS

Jeff Horan (Editor)
Jari Kolterman (Editor)
Martin Laydon (Photographer)
Katherine S. Parker (Photographer)
Kimberly Jo Peterson (Editor)
Shelby W. Shrigley (Editor)

INDEX

BOOKS FOR YOUNG READERS AGES 8 AND UP

from John Muir Publications

X-ray Vision Series

*E*ach title in the series is 8¹/₂" x 11", 48 pages, $9.95, paperback, with four-color photographs and illustrations and written by Ron Schultz.

Looking Inside the Brain
Looking Inside Cartoon Animation
Looking Inside Sports Aerodynamics
Looking Inside Sunken Treasure
Looking Inside Telescopes and the Night Sky

Masters of Motion Series

*E*ach title in the series is 10¹/₄" x 9", 48 pages, $9.95, paperback, with four-color photographs and illustrations.

How to Drive an Indy Race Car
David Rubel

How to Fly a 747
Tim Paulson

How to Fly the Space Shuttle
Russell Shorto

The "Extremely Weird" Series

*A*ll of the titles are written by Sarah Lovett, 8¹/₂" x 9", 48 pages, and $9.95 paperbacks.

Extremely Weird Bats
Extremely Weird Birds
Extremely Weird Endangered Species
Extremely Weird Fishes
Extremely Weird Frogs
Extremely Weird Insects
Extremely Weird Primates
Extremely Weird Reptiles
Extremely Weird Sea Creatures
Extremely Weird Spiders

Other Titles of Interest

Habitats
Where the Wild Things Live
Randi Hacker and Jackie Kaufman
8¹/₂" x 11", 48 pages, color illustrations, $9.95 paper

The Indian Way
Learning to Communicate with Mother Earth
Gary McLain
Painting by Gary McLain
Illustrations by Michael Taylor
7" x 9", 114 pages, two-color illustrations, $9.95, paper

Kids Explore America's African-American Heritage
Westridge Young Writers Workshop
7" x 9", 118 pages, illustrations and photographs, $8.95, paper

Kids Explore America's Hispanic Heritage
Westridge Young Writers Workshop
7" x 9", 112 pages, illustrations and photographs, $7.95, paper

Rads, Ergs, and Cheeseburgers
The Kids' Guide to Energy and the Environment
Bill Yanda
Illustrated by Michael Taylor
7" x 9", 108 pages, two-color illustrations, $13.95, paper

The Kids' Environment Book
What's Awry and Why
Anne Pedersen
Illustrated by Sally Blakemore
7" x 9", 192 pages, two-color illustrations, $13.95, paper

The Quill Hedgehog Adventures Series

Green fiction for young readers. Each title is written by John Waddington-Feather and illustrated by Doreen Edmond.

Quill's Adventures in the Great Beyond
BOOK ONE
5¹/₂" x 8¹/₂", 96 pages, $5.95, paper

Quill's Adventures in Wasteland
BOOK TWO
5¹/₂" x 8¹/₂", 132 pages, $5.95, paper

Quill's Adventures in Grozzieland
BOOK THREE
5¹/₂" x 8¹/₂", 132 pages, $5.95, paper

The Kidding Around Travel Guides

All of the titles listed below are 64 pages and $9.95 except for *Kidding Around the National Parks* and *Kidding Around Spain*, which are 108 pages and $12.95.

"A combination of practical information, vital statistics, and historical asides."

—New York Times

Kidding Around Atlanta
Kidding Around Boston, 2nd ed.
Kidding Around Chicago, 2nd ed.
Kidding Around the Hawaiian Islands,
Kidding Around London
Kidding Around Los Angeles
Kidding Around the National Parks of the Southwest
Kidding Around New York City, 2nd ed.
Kidding Around Paris
Kidding Around Philadelphia
Kidding Around San Diego
Kidding Around San Francisco

Kidding Around Santa Fe
Kidding Around Seattle
Kidding Around Spain
Kidding Around Washington, D.C., 2nd ed.

ORDERING INFORMATION

If you send us money for a book not yet available, we will hold your money until we can ship you the book. Your books will be sent to you via UPS (for U.S. destinations). UPS will not deliver to a P.O. Box; please give us a street address. Include $3.75 for the first item ordered and $.50 for each additional item to cover shipping and handling costs. For air-mail within the U.S., enclose $4.00. All foreign orders will be shipped surface rate; please enclose $3.00 for the first item and $1.00 for each additional item. Please inquire about foreign air-mail rates.

METHOD OF PAYMENT

Your order may be paid by check, money order, or credit card. We cannot be responsible for cash sent through the mail. All payments must be made in U.S. dollars drawn on a U.S. bank. Canadian postal money orders in U.S. dollars are acceptable. For VISA, MasterCard, or American Express orders, include your card number, expiration date, and your signature, or call (800) 888-7504. Books ordered on American Express cards can be shipped only to the billing address of the cardholder. Sorry, no C.O.D.'s. Residents of sunny New Mexico, add 5.875% tax to the total.

Address all orders and inquiries to:
John Muir Publications
P.O. Box 613
Santa Fe, NM 87504
(505) 982-4078
(800) 888-7504

SEA CREATURES